MAD SCIENTISTS NEED LOVE TOO

BERLYNN WOHL

CARNATION BOOKS

ISBN (ebook): 978-1-948272-26-1

ISBN (paperback): 978-1-948272-22-3

Published 2019 by Carnation Books

CarnationBooks.com

contact@carnationbooks.com

Seattle, WA, USA

For Rael, my personal consultant on all things to do with mad science.

CONTENTS

AND THEN THERE WAS THE ONE ABOUT...

THE SPACE-FARING WRITER

HAVING RECENTLY RETURNED from a harrowing trip to outer space, Bell took his memoir to a publisher. The publisher was astounded by his tales of adventure.

"There's just one problem," the publisher said, "and it's with the title."

Bell put hand to his mouth. "Oh, should I have come up with something a little less forward than *I Fucked An Alien*?"

"That's not the problem," the publisher said. "The thing is, these days everyone wants books that have a self-help aspect to them. Readers need to feel like they've taken something useful away, and not just been entertained."

"Got it," said Bell. "Then let's call it *How I Fucked An Alien*."

THE HEIST

AARON PAID for his drink with cash. He paid for everything with cash. He was old-fashioned – at least, that's how he would explain it to anyone who pointed it out. The truth was, other people's cash was a lot less risky than other people's plastic, and anyway, he'd never been much of a computer guy.

He kept an eye on the place while he drank his beer, considering whether he should eat dinner here at the bar, where the food would be terrible but no one would notice him, or whether he should head further into town, where he could get a good steak but where he would stick out more for dining alone. He was no stranger to finding company on short notice, but he tended to do that only *after* pulling off a job, when the thrill of a bag full of jewels and cash made him long for a certain type of companionship, someone to burn off the adrenaline with. He wouldn't know what to say to someone for a full hour across a dinner table.

Aaron wasn't usually so indecisive, but as he watched his fellow patrons move around the bar, it seemed like something odd was going on, and he was compelled to stay and puzzle it out. It took him the entire beer to realize what it was: just at the time of night when a bar ought to be filling up, this one was emptying out. Plays on the jukebox got more sporadic; groups who looked like they would have settled in for the evening finished one drink apiece and then made their way out, and all this at – Aaron checked his watch – eight-thirty, no less.

"Every Saturday night like this?" Aaron said to the bartender when he came around again.

"Thank Christ, no," the bartender said. "Tonight everyone's going out into the goddamn desert for some bullshit."

"Aliens," said a patron at the bar, a man who had the look of someone just waiting for the slightest bit of attention, so he could pour out all his heartfelt tales. Every bar had one. He looked to Aaron, waiting to be asked to elaborate.

Aaron was game. "Aliens?"

"Couple months ago on a Saturday night some college kids went out past the city limits to fool around on a lover's lane, and the next day they swore up and down that while they were out there, they saw a flying saucer. Of course no one believed them, 'cause they were dumb kids. But then exactly two weeks later, a girl got dumped on the side of the road by her angry boyfriend, and when she got back to town, she said she'd seen the same flying saucer, zipping around in the sky. But she admitted that she'd done a little of that, what do you call it, MGM? KMFDM? That drug the kids are all into these days. So no one thought twice about what she said. But then one of the richy-riches saw one, near the same stretch of road where the kids and the girl saw it. And at the same time, on a Saturday night. Of course everyone believed *him*, even though those rich assholes do more drugs than any of us." He swirled the remainder of his drink around as he said this with a sneer. "So tonight everyone's going out to that spot in the desert, waiting to see the flying saucer."

"Sounds pretty exciting," Aaron said. "So why aren't you going?"

The man stared at Aaron with one raised eyebrow. "Because aliens aren't real." He turned back to his drink. "Probably just some kids playing with the goddamn drones their parents got 'em for Christmas."

Aaron downed the last of his beer and got up from the bar. "Well, I've been thinking about getting one of those things, they look fun.

I'm gonna head out there and see if one of those spoiled brats will let me take theirs for a test drive." He slipped his coat back on and said, "You gentlemen have a nice night."

Aaron was experienced enough at his profession not to let his excitement get the better of him when he stumbled upon an opportunity this good. He got in his car and drove towards the center of town, slowing down as he rolled by the nicest restaurants with the biggest windows, peering in. Just like the run-down bar, they were nearly empty. Whatever this UFO really was, it was drawing this resort town's well-heeled out into the desert, too. Rows and rows of houses left unoccupied for hours. Fantastic. Aaron had only planned on passing through, but his Saturday night had just become fully booked.

Aaron headed for the incongruously wooded neighborhood on the other side of downtown; folks in this part of the country just loved to plant cypress trees and other Mediterranean plants, to make their patch of desert wasteland feel more like Tuscany. He tucked his car into a discreet spot at the edge of the neighborhood and made his way through the shadows on foot, so that he would not draw the attention of the numerous drivers making their way uniformly in the other direction.

These houses were all new enough to have central air, which meant no window air conditioning units to simply shove aside around here. That also meant that there would likely not be any doors or windows left open a crack to fight the desert heat – the absolute easiest targets, in Aaron's line of work.

But there were always back doors left unlocked, especially when the last person through them was a careless child, and *especially* especially when the parents felt secure enough about having a backyard that was difficult to access that they got lazy about correcting the child's oversight. Aaron vaulted a gate, then crawled through a hedge, looking for one of these unlocked doors. No luck. Perhaps there had been some local infiltration recently, and that had gotten everyone on their guard.

But then, Aaron heard the sound of a garage door opening. He darted through a side yard, careful to stay in the shadows, and sure enough, right next door, an enormous SUV was trundling out of a three-car garage. The vehicle paused a moment, so that the driver could hit the button to close the garage door, but then it backed into the street and hurried off, with the door still dropping. Aaron dove out of the shadows and under the door, feeling not a little like the type of action-movie hero who flung himself around the jungle in search of ancient treasures.

The door inside the garage that led to the house was unlocked – no surprise there. Aaron went inside, finding himself in the den of a well-appointed contemporary split-level. The furniture was sleek and modern, and the art objects scattered around were weird and abstract. Aaron was confident that he had plenty of time to look around, but in case he didn't, he stuck to his usual routine, and headed straight for the master bedroom.

Climbing the stairs, he looked at the photographs that lined each wall, searching for clues as to what he might find. The most recent pictures showed a husband, wife, and three children, the youngest an infant. The wife wore a chunky necklace full of stones in one formal photo; Aaron would have to keep an eye out for it. The rest of the photos showed ostentatious possessions that meant nothing to Aaron – in one, horses that were probably stabled nearby; in another, a boat named *Vanessa*, in front of which the husband was standing, with what was presumably a fishing buddy, both of them red with sunburn. Between them hung an enormous marlin.

At the top of the stairs, the hallway was lit only by the moon, thanks to a skylight overhead. Aaron saw three doors on the left side, but only two on the right. He figured the master bedroom was one of those two, and made for the first door. In the darkness, he bumped right into someone who was on their way out.

Frozen in place by shock, they looked each other up and down. Aaron determined quickly that this was not a member of the household – no one in any of the photographs had been five feet tall, wearing a skin-tight silver bodysuit, with green skin and huge shiny black eyes peering out of an enormous round skull.

"What are you doing here?" the alien said, clearly in a panic.

"Me? What the hell are *you* doing here? I'm only not supposed to be in this *house*. You're not supposed to be on this *planet!*"

"Don't act so high and mighty with me! I'm here on important business." The alien indicated himself, then pointed accusingly at Aaron. "You're clearly just here to rob the place."

The accusation was spot-on, but Aaron refused to be intimidated. "How do you know I'm here to rob the place?"

"You're wearing a mask and carrying a sack. Are you going to try to convince me you're here to hook up the cable?"

Whoever this alien was, this was not his first time on Earth, apparently. "Okay, fine," Aaron said, "but what's *your* important business?"

"Part of my ship is in this house," the alien explained, "and I have to get it back."

"What do you mean, part of your ship? Are these people aliens too? Like, rival aliens?"

The alien sighed at all the questions. "I was a couple hundred miles north of here when I had an engine malfunction, which blew part of the hull from my ship. It fell into the desert, and then some idiot picked it up, made a sculpture out of it, and sold it to *these* people at Burning Man."

Of all things, it was the final part of the alien's story that Aaron now found incredulous. "You can't sell anything at Burning Man."

The alien put his hands up and sneered, "Fine, the guy 'gifted' my hull to them, and then they, coincidentally, immediately gifted him a bicycle and a case of vodka. Now, I spent months convincing everyone in the neighborhood to scram for the night so I can grab this thing, so can you help me? I don't know how much time I–"

Just then, a key clicked in a lock at the bottom of the stairs, and the front door swung open. The alien grabbed Aaron by the arm and pulled him into the master bedroom. They stood still and listened for a moment, until they heard two sets of footsteps coming up the stairs. Aaron pointed at the walk-in closet, and they both darted inside and shut the door.

A light came on in the hall, and now Aaron could see that the door to the closet had angled slats, through which he could see into the bedroom. For a moment, he felt exposed, but then realized he was actually at an advantage, because he could see out but no one in the bedroom could see into the closet, where it was still dark. Beside him, the alien was perfectly still and silent.

Two men came into view. Aaron recognized them from the photos on the wall: one was the father from the family photographs, and the other was the fishing buddy. As they tumbled onto the king-size bed together, tugging at each other's clothes, Aaron had to contain a laugh of surprise at this obviously clandestine encounter. But as things went on, and the now-naked men began to clutch at each other and rub against each other in earnest, Aaron felt a pang of envy: he'd had his share of frantic, thrilling interludes with other men, but these two, with their happy sighs and occasional giggles, were clearly long-time companions enjoying an opportunity that they had both been anticipating for a while.

One of them flopped onto his other side, so that they could sixty-nine, and they went at it with such relish, such joy, but also with a confidence that came with familiarity. When you knew someone's body, knew their preferences, even an occasional fumble was sweetened by laughter and tenderness.

The alien tugged on Aaron's sleeve, pulling him from his reverie, and Aaron leaned down, so the alien could whisper to him. "What are they doing? What is this?"

"They're having sex," Aaron explained.

"Nuh-uh," said the alien. "I read the entire manual on humans, including the part on sex, and it never mentioned anything that looked like that."

"Then you need to get a better manual," Aaron hissed. "Do your people not do stuff like this?"

The alien shook his head. "We don't even have genitals. We're produced in vats in a laboratory, so we don't need them."

"Jesus. What do you do for fun back home?"

"Not a lot. That's why I left."

"Okay, okay, *shhh.*" Aaron was pretty sure they were being quiet enough that the two men would not hear them over their own moans and sighs, but he didn't want to take any chances. Also, he didn't want to be distracted by chatting; he wanted to watch these two men fucking right in front of him, because it was intensely hot.

One of the two men, the husband, pulled away and rolled over to the nightstand, where he fished around until he found a bottle of lube. "Yes, *yes*," the other one growled, and got on his hands and knees.

By this time, Aaron was achingly hard, and he would probably have been jerking off if he didn't have company in the closet. But it was probably better this way; getting caught would be a disaster in any case, but getting caught with his dick in his hand would have been another thing entirely. As it was, he thought about how, assuming he got away clean from this situation, he was absolutely going to pick up a guy somewhere afterwards, at the earliest possible moment. It would just be some stranger, though, not a good friend and longtime companion, not like what these guys had. Just someone he would never see again, someone he wouldn't really be able to share that much with.

Not that his dick cared right now. As the two men grunted and groaned and pounded away, Aaron's longing for companionship became more and more a longing for a good deep fuck, under any circumstances which might be available.

When they finished, the two men lolled together on the bed for just a few minutes in blissful silence, until the husband said, "We probably should go. I told Vanessa I was just coming back to grab my good camera. If I'm not back soon, she'll be wondering what's up."

"Guess you're right," the fishing buddy said, and rolled off the bed and to his feet. They dressed and left, their footsteps fading as they trotted down the stairs. When Aaron was sure he'd heard the front door open and shut, he heaved a sigh. "Holy shit," he whispered.

"That was a close one," the alien said. "But I've had closer. Now, any chance you could help me get that piece of my ship?"

"Sorry, I don't have the time. I've got my own business here."

"Oh yeah? What is it you want? The cash? The jewelry?" The alien pointed at the safe in the corner of the closet.

"As a matter of fact, yeah. I'll need all the time I can get to crack that safe."

The alien revealed, in his hand, a blunt metal wand, which he waved at the safe. The dial spun, and then the door clicked open.

Without pausing to ask about the wand, Aaron dug in, grabbing a stack of cash and a velvet box – probably with that necklace inside – and shoving it into his bag. He pushed some papers aside and grabbed two automatic pistols as well; he could easily fence those.

He stood up, closed the safe, and spun the dial. The alien said, "Okay, *now* will you help me?"

Well, it was only fair. "You got it," Aaron said.

The alien described the general shape of the thing he was looking for, and they split up, searching each room. Aaron saw a lot of wacky sculptures, but none of them had any parts that seemed to match what he was looking for.

Finally, from downstairs, he heard the alien call out, "Found it!" Just off the den, there was a little room being used as a home office, and in it, the alien was looking grimly at a sculpture in the corner. It appeared to be just a lot of found junk, welded together at wild angles, the sort of thing a rich asshole would think was art.

"This is not good," the alien said, pointing. The jagged piece of his ship's hull, the largest part of the sculpture, was planted in a slab of concrete. "I thought I was going to be able to just cut it out with this." He held up the strange wand. "But it only works on metal."

"You can't cut it out just from like, right here?" Aaron indicated the spot where the corner of the hull met the concrete.

"I need the whole piece, or I can't leave this planet's atmosphere." They stood in silence for a minute. The alien seemed like he was deep in thought, so Aaron tried to look like he was thinking of a solution too, even though he had no idea what was going on.

Finally, the alien said, "I've got some tools on my ship to dissolve the concrete, but I can't bring them out here. They're embedded in the ship itself. This whole thing has got to go on board."

"Where's the ship?"

The alien pointed vaguely. "In the backyard. It's cloaked."

Aaron got a solid grip on the sculpture and rocked it back and forth a little. "It's pretty heavy, but together we could probably get it out there."

They struggled for several minutes, pivoting and rocking the sculpture across the room – the carpet made it difficult to drag. They directed each other, encouraged each other, and got it halfway across the den when Aaron had an idea. "Okay, you can't dislodge the hull from the concrete, but you don't need this whole thing, do you? Just the part that's your ship?"

"Right."

"So why drag all this other crap? Can you use your device to cut away all this other metal?"

"Oh, yeah! Why didn't I think of that?" The alien waved the metal wand around, slicing away chunks of the sculpture, until it was just the hull and a few stray bits of re-bar that had been welded on, plus the slab of concrete. Aaron looked at the detritus on the floor; it would be a lot more obvious a lot sooner to this family that they had been robbed; but he would be here all night otherwise, exhausting himself with dragging the whole thing. The going was much easier now, and they soon had the hull through the patio doors and into the backyard.

The alien gave Aaron specific instructions about where to move and how to drag the sculpture to get it onto the ship, which was still cloaked. "Duck your head here. Okay, to the right, three more steps, and–no, don't! *Oof*, sorry, I did tell you to duck."

"I didn't know I had to *keep* ducking!" Aaron said, rubbing the back of his head. "How much farther?"

"Not far, you're on the ramp. Step up now."

The ship seemed to materialize as Aaron was stepping up into it. It wasn't a particularly spacious vessel; there was enough room for them to stand with the remains of the sculpture, but not much more. All around the circular room were dials and screens and compartments. The alien sat in a swooping chair in front of several panels of buttons and began pressing some. There didn't appear to be a seat available, so Aaron clutched a sturdy handle on the wall and held on while the ship took off.

"I'm just going to take us out of town a little ways," the alien said, "to somewhere I can work on the ship while it's de-cloaked."

Aaron watched on a viewscreen as the ground got further and further away; soon, houses were zipping by beneath them. Despite these strange surroundings, the feeling that washed over Aaron in that moment was very familiar: the relief that came with a bag filled with loot and a clean getaway. But that was almost an afterthought, now – successfully stealing a huge piece of alien technology was much more satisfying, even if from a practical standpoint it was far less useful to him than the contents of the safe. He was erect again, his body conditioned to get ready for the activity he usually pursued next.

"Do you think you could – hey, I never got your name, by the way," Aaron said.

The alien was occupied with the control panel. "Oh, uh, you can call me Taq."

"Cool, Taq, got it." Aaron looked at the viewscreen; they were touching down somewhere in the desert. How far they had traveled, he had no idea. "So, can you drop me by my car at some point? I've got, uh, one more errand to run tonight."

"Sure thing." The ship settled on the ground, and after Taq flicked a final switch, things got quiet. "But first, I thought I might repay you for the favor you did me." He got out of his seat and walked over to Aaron.

Aaron let go of the handle he'd been gripping and held up the bag. "No need. This was an excellent take, thanks for helping with the safe."

"That was nothing, though." Taq took one more step towards him; he couldn't be any closer now. "I feel like there's something else I can do, to show you my gratitude."

Whether Taq was unaware of or simply unconcerned with the pace of human intimacy, Aaron did not know. But the moment he felt

Taq's hand caressing his cock through his trousers, he jumped back. "Oh, uh, you don't have to..." he began. But part of him was saying, *Finally*.

Aaron made no further protest when Taq did not retreat; twice he'd said it was not necessary, so if Taq wanted to show his gratitude by following the example of those two men back at the house, well, it was out of Aaron's hands, wasn't it?

Taq closed the distance between them again. He unzipped Aaron's trousers, and his cock sprang out, so rigid and in need of attention that it twitched with each beat of his heart. Taq took hold of it, and when he did, they gasped in unison. Taq began to stroke it, first slow, then fast, and Aaron looked around for that handle to hold onto. His knees shook with the relief of finally being touched – and the shock over the strange being who was doing it.

"Is it good?" Taq inquired "Am I doing it right?"

Breathless, Aaron nodded.

"I have a bunk," Taq offered.

"That would be great, yeah, 'cause I'm about to fall over."

Taq pressed a button, and a bed unfolded from the wall. Aaron fell flat on his back onto it, and Taq immediately set to work stripping him of all his clothes. "We don't have to make it a big production," Aaron said. "Just a handjob would be fine." Taq ignored him.

When Aaron was naked, Taq peeled off his own silver suit, revealing a smooth, featureless body – no nipples, nothing between his legs. He pressed himself against Aaron, rubbing their bodies together. His skin was satiny-soft; he seemed to almost glide against Aaron. Aaron's cock found the smooth space between Taq's legs, and began to rock up into it. Taq shivered, and squeezed his thighs together, letting Aaron grind hungrily. The sensation was familiar but strange, as Taq's body was so smooth, and much lighter and more nimble than a human's.

Aaron cradled Taq's behind, moving him to dictate the rhythm. He knew that was a bit selfish, though, so he whispered, "This is amazing. But what can I do for you?"

"You're doing it," Taq said, a tremor in his voice as he rocked.

"When I touch someone else, I can feel the sensations they feel. So making you feel good makes me feel good."

Aaron slowed his rhythm as this information sank in. In a strange way, this might have been the most deeply arousing revelation he'd ever heard. "So we're like, really *connected* right now, huh?"

"Yes."

"Yeah," Aaron said, "we are." He breathed deep, trying to regroup. As he rolled his hips, he relished the pressure of Taq's velvety skin, and watched Taq close his eyes and gasp. He kept it slow, basking in the sweet warmth of it, a kind of tenderness he had never experienced before. His thighs began to quiver, as this simplest of ways of seeking physical pleasure against the body of another turned into an exhilarating mutual delight.

Taq pressed himself head-to-toe against Aaron's body, never lifting his hands from Aaron's muscled arms. Intoxicated by their shared pleasure, Aaron thought he might melt right into the bed. It was so wonderfully indulgent, knowing that the person he was taking to bed wanted to feel all of him, not just the brief friction required to get off in a hurry. There was a beating heart pressed against his own – or some kind of thumping organ in Taq's chest, for sure – and Aaron wrapped his arms around Taq to hold him tight, to feel it even closer.

The heat in his belly grew urgent, and no matter how he tried to slow down, breathe deep, the effortless rhythm they shared was driving him out of control with excitement. "Listen," he gasped, "I'm gonna come soon. Is this your first time doing this with a human?"

"It is."

"Get ready, then, because it's kind of intense."

Taq nodded, and continued squeezing him just right. Aaron's hips surged, his body – and then Taq's body – bursting with crackling energy. Their mutual cries pierced the quiet darkness of the ship's interior. Aaron thrashed through an unbearable deluge of pulsing ecstasy as he spilled between Taq's thighs. Even as his climax ebbed, he continued to clutch at Taq's body, sharing the thrumming yet tender intimacy of two damp, trembling bodies pressed against one another. He'd had a whole world of need inside him, and he only understood that now, having finally satisfied it.

"That was fun," Taq mumbled against Aaron's shoulder. He sounded about as relaxed and sleepy as Aaron felt. "Can we do it again?"

Aaron laughed. "I'll need like twenty minutes. And a nap."

Taq relaxed his body, and Aaron rested a hand on his back, stroking Taq's soft skin as he drifted to sleep.

When Aaron woke up, he was alone. He sat up and swung around, putting his feet on the floor, looking for his clothes. They had been folded up and put at the foot of the bunk. Just then, the door to the ramp opened up, and Taq appeared. He was dressed in his silver suit again. "Got the hull fixed," he said cheerfully. "Sorry I left you, but when you fell asleep I started to feel funny, so I had to get up off of you."

"No problem." Aaron ran one hand through his mussed hair. "I suppose now that your ship's fixed, you're going to leave Earth?"

"Hmm, probably. Did you still want me to drop you at your car?"

Aaron felt a bit bereft, but dared not reveal this. "I guess so," was his reply.

"Okay. But maybe let's make one more stop first."

Taq flew the ship across town and down the highway, back into the desert. Aaron watched through the viewscreen, and soon saw below them a huge crowd of people: everyone who had come out to see the flying saucer.

"There's all your townsfolk," Taq said.

Aaron laughed, "No, I'm not from here. Just passing through."

"I see. Well, before I drop you off, you want to give these guys a cheap thrill?"

Aaron laughed. "Is that okay?"

Taq looked at him, his eyes still big and black but now looking perhaps a little more sly. "How many stories have you read about people seeing strange things in the sky?"

"Lots."

"And how often did you see any follow-up? Anyone even getting close to solving the mystery?"

Aaron thought for a second. "I guess pretty much never."

"Exactly. Let's do this." Taq uncloaked his ship, just for a second, before he sped off, then cloaked once more and headed for the nice part of town. Aaron caught the briefest glimpse on the viewscreen of a sea of awed faces...followed by a few gunshots. "Why do idiots always want to shoot at things they see in the sky," he heard Taq mutter.

Taq landed the ship in an empty parking lot near Aaron's car. Aaron picked up his bag and looked at Taq. "I guess this is goodbye," he said. He shuffled a little, not making much of an effort to head for the door.

"I guess so," Taq replied, making no effort whatsoever to hurry him along.

"Listen, uh, this was a fun night." Aaron was trying to think of anything to say, to make this a better farewell. "I'll never forget it. Sorry if I was rude to you at first."

Taq made a dismissive gesture. "It's alright. We really surprised each other, didn't we?"

They laughed a little. Taq fidgeted.

"You know," Taq said, "you could come with me...if you want."

It was all Aaron could do not to immediately drop the bag and get settled in again. "Are you sure? I don't want to make any trouble for you."

"It's no trouble," Taq insisted. "I'm on my own out here, and it can get lonely."

Aaron had not gotten as far as he had in life, though, making decisions headlong. He bit his lip. "Is it safe for a human? I don't have a space suit or anything. And I have to eat. Is there food I can eat out there?"

Taq shrugged. "We can just go places that it's cool for humans to go, and where there's food humans can eat."

"Well, then there's not really any reason for me to stay here," Aaron said, gazing at the viewscreen, which showed his unremarkable car tucked away in an unremarkable lot in an unremarkable town. “It was only ever about the cheap thrills, I guess.” He hefted the bag full of cash and guns.

“Lots of stuff to steal in space,” Taq offered, “if that’s your thing.”

Aaron sat on the still-unfolded bunk and gestured to Taq to return to the pilot’s seat. “I guess we’ll see what my new thing is, in space.”

THIS ONE'S WEIRDER

QUINN DID NOT bother to ask Erick if he wanted hot chocolate with mint chocolate chip ice cream in it; after dinner, he just brought two steaming mugs over to the sofa, where Erik was reading on his tablet, and explained to Erick that he must want some, because it was the most amazingly delicious thing in the world.

"Why thank you, my darling," Erick said, carefully taking the mug from Quinn's hand. Quinn plopped down next to him on the sofa. Erick tried to return his full attention to his reading, but before he could do so, Quinn took a deep breath, like he'd been waiting for the perfect opportunity to say something.

"What do you think of toys?" Quinn asked, as he scooped a spoonful of ice cream out of the hot chocolate.

Erick stared at Quinn blankly for several seconds.

"I mean, sex toys," Quinn clarified.

"Oh, that's much better; your initial question seemed strangely vast and open-ended." Erick stirred his hot chocolate, to melt the ice cream some more, so it would be cool enough to drink without burning his tongue. "I must confess that I haven't given an enormous amount of thought to them, but...I suppose this is actually a question about incorporating toys into our relationship."

"Yeah."

"Alright, then." Erick paused to take a sip, then said, "While I am not highly motivated to acquire or use any myself, I'm not opposed to you doing so, as I can't imagine myself feeling threatened in any way by them. I am confident that you find me a satisfactory partner, and that I could not be replaced by a toy."

"That's true!" Quinn said, pointing at Erick, always excited whenever Erick was being agreeable. "No toy could ever argue with me about whether *Firefly* would have stayed good if it had gotten like ten seasons."

"I meant that I provide you with affection and attention," Erick replied, "which a toy cannot. But, whatever keeps you by my side, I suppose."

"So if I wanted to bring one to bed, say, tomorrow night, that would be alright?"

Erick seemed unconcerned, blithely sipping from his mug. "I don't see why not," he said.

"Cool, cool. And what if I wanted to bring, like, five, that I acquired before we got together. What about that?"

This made Erick pause for a moment, but again, he shrugged and said, "I feel powerless to stop you."

Quinn nodded. "Cool, cool."

The following night, Erick found himself sitting fully dressed – minus his tie and Oxfords – on the bed next to a completely naked Quinn, examining an oddly-shaped and multi-colored dildo up-close through his glasses. On a nearby towel sat a bottle of lube and four more dildos, each of them wildly different in color, shape, and size.

"This one is much smaller than the others," Erick remarked on the slender pearlescent model in his hand.

Quinn was unfolding another towel, and tucking it beneath himself. "Oh yeah, uh, I don't like trying to get my fingers in myself, the angle is kind of awkward, so that little one is to kind of get me started."

"That's very sensible. By the way, am I supposed to still be clothed for this?"

"Uh-huh. I want you to be fully dressed while I'm naked. Definitely keep the glasses on, too."

"Alright. And so I'm to go in order by size?"

"Yeah," Quinn said. When Erick seemed to be having trouble arranging two of the toys by size, because their variance was more in their shape, he helped by placing the one that was a tentacle fourth in the order.

Erick picked up the one that was to come last. Marbled taxi-yellow and orange in color, it was of a formidable size starting from the very tip, but the bulge near the base was what startled him. He could not get his hand around the thickness of that part.

"What is this?" he asked, alarmed. "Is this supposed to be like what dogs have?"

"Maybe a little, yeah."

"Have you put all of this one inside yourself before?"

Quinn blushed. "Uh, not all of it? I was hoping maybe you could help. When we get to that one."

Quinn laid down on his back with his knees bent and his legs slightly spread, and Erick situated himself at the edge of the bed beside him. The toys and the lube Erick set on the nightstand, so they would not roll around or get jostled – Erick did *not* want to have to stop the proceedings because one of these things rolled under the bed and got covered in dust bunnies.

Erick picked up the first dildo again, the modest affair. It smoothly transitioned from a shapely glans to a prominent coronal ridge, with just a few gentle swells in the shaft to keep it interesting. Erick had never thought about acquiring a toy for himself, but he imagined that, if he were gifted something like this, it would probably be the last one he would ever own, as it seemed like everything he could possibly need. But, Quinn was a little different. Much more adventurous.

Erick drizzled lube on the toy. Though the angle of approach was different than he was used to, it was no great task to align it with Quinn's body more or less as he would his own penis, and once he'd done so, he gave it a gentle push.

Quinn easily welcomed this charming intruder. His softened expression and happy humming reminded Erick of all the times he had serviced Quinn this way with his own body, and so he began to think that this situation was not so bizarre as it had first appeared. The toy seemed to evoke all the usual sparks of pleasure, as Erick settled into a leisurely rhythm with it.

But such simple delights did not keep Quinn interested for long, not tonight anyway. "Okay, I'm ready for the next one," he said.

Erick dutifully removed the toy and placed it on the towel. Then he reached for the second one in the order. This one was bright red, and had much more heft to it. It's flexible shaft was composed of stacked ridges, and the glans narrowed dramatically at the tip – easier to insert, but Erick found it difficult to believe that it was comfortable to have inside. But Quinn was begging for Erick to hurry up and put it in, so Erick deferred to his judgment.

Beyond the narrow tip, this toy was slightly more challenging, and Quinn wriggled as he accepted it, tugging at his cock the way he often did to help himself relax when he was being penetrated. Erick was mesmerized by the sight of each thick, ridged segment disappearing one after another into Quinn's eager hole. It was definitely different from what his own prick looked like going inside, and Quinn's reaction was far more exuberant. Erick was riveted to what he was doing – it was so filthy and exciting – but at the same time, he couldn't help but feel just a touch insecure.

When the toy was all the way in to the base, Quinn heaved a sigh and looked to Erick. He must have noticed Erick's ambiguous expression, and so tried to soothe him: "Sorry that this is kind of all about me. I owe you a big one in return for this."

Erick snapped out of his erotic haze and quickly said, "Think nothing of it. Your pleasure is a delight to witness."

And this was the truth. Two days ago, if he had been given a list of potential bedroom activities to pursue with Quinn, "Penetrate Quinn with strange toys while remaining fully clothed" would likely have been relegated to the bottom of that list. But to his surprise, Erick found that despite a pang of intimidation, he really was enjoying himself right now. What would not have occurred to him, perusing that hypothetical list, was that this encounter contained all his favorite things about their private time: a little bit of sweet, quiet intimacy, before Quinn got loud; Quinn being very squirmy and obvious about his pleasure; and the ego boost it gave Erick, knowing that he was making Quinn feel good in a way no one else was allowed to.

In fact, this last thing he felt more keenly now, perhaps, than ever before, because this particular activity allowed him to really focus on Quinn's pleasure. When they made love, Erick was distracted by what he was experiencing, and when he was performing oral sex, he was concentrating on the task. But here, while exerting minimal effort, just a few flicks of the wrist, Erick could watch Quinn's face and body as much as he liked, enjoying the sight of perspiration springing up on Quinn's chest as he rocked and cooed, telling Erick, with or without words, all about how nice it felt.

Now that it was all the way in, Quinn indicated that Erick should pause for a moment, so that he could just enjoy for a while the feeling of being stuffed with a large and unusual cock. Erick kept his hand on the base, but held it still. "What do you think about when you are using..." Erick did not want to say the world *dildo* aloud if he could possibly help it. "...Using these things, by yourself?"

Quinn's hand on his own prick slowed, as he thought about the question. "Oh, uh, I kind of would try to imagine that I was getting gang-banged by monsters. Like I was at their mercy, and I had to take all their monster dicks. But, it's kind of hard to sustain that fantasy when you have to, you know, lube them all up yourself, one at a time, and put them in yourself, you know?"

Erick was always pleased when Quinn was candid with him, but he wasn't sure what to do with this information. "Would you like me to, ah, help you with this fantasy? Am I ruining it by talking? Should I maybe growl a little, like a monster?"

Quinn laughed. "Nah, man. I actually kind of...I'm kind of into what's happening right now. I'm butt-naked while you're looking all prim and proper and putting dildos in my ass. And you're doing it because you love me and stuff and want to make me happy. That's a turn-on, too."

Erick put his free hand to his face, to cover up how red he was getting. It was exciting for him, as well, to see Quinn sprawled naked on the bed, and to be in a position himself where he had to remain clear-headed and restrained, so that he could administer the pleasure.

At Quinn's urging, Erick resumed guiding the dildo in and out of Quinn's body. He was careful not to give Quinn too much too quickly, though Quinn soon made it clear that if anything, he was having the opposite problem. "Give me the next one," he demanded.

Whereas the previous toy had been more reptilian in appearance, this one fell strongly into an alien aesthetic, with it's metallic gray color, strange spiraling veins, and slightly asymmetrical bumps, all of which made it look oddly muscular. It was also dotted with rows of prominent nubs, which even Erick had to admit looked intriguing; he imagined they would feel very interesting going in and out.

There was already lots of lube in and around Quinn's hole, but Erick saw no reason to be stingy with it. He spread some more over the strange thing in his hand, watching Quinn's face light up with lustful anticipation.

Quinn's red, wet rim had to stretch a little more to take this one, rolling over the bulbous crown and gripping each curve of the shaft, and he fidgeted as all the little bumps tugged at him. Erick teased him especially with this one, giving just a little at a time, then drawing it nearly all the way back out before giving it again, a fraction deeper each time.

Erick listened carefully to Quinn's hitching breath, watched his thighs shake and his toes curl, and asked, "Do you like how much I'm giving you?"

Quinn sobbed a little when he nodded, then said, "Is that all of it?"

Erick took a closer look. "Just a little more," he replied, and nudged the last of it in, so that the wide base brushed the backs of Quinn's thighs. "There we are."

Quinn's hair was stuck to his forehead where it was damp with sweat. His breaths were choppy, his body twitching, and so Erick decided to take a little rest, letting Quinn calm down and get used to the fullness nestled inside him. The effect of the toy was so powerful, Quinn had stopped touching himself – he sort of tried one more time after taking a break, but quickly took his hand away, clearly overstimulated. Erick watched the way the pre-come gathered at the tip of Quinn's cock, and dribbled down at intervals onto his hip or thigh. With every twitch and jerk of his body, Quinn was making the alien toy press against his prostate, coaxing out more warm little spills of fluid.

"Can I tell you more about the monster fantasy?" Quinn said, his voice barely above a whisper.

"Of course, please do."

"So the monsters have this hunger that can only be satisfied by my body, but I'm so little, they have to take turns. Only one can fuck my hole at a time, but I also have my mouth, plus I have my hands. So I can actually take four monsters at once." Quinn's voice got higher, and more frenzied, as he went on. "I've got one fucking me, I'm sucking another one off, and I'm jerking off two more. And even though I'm little, they start to really like me, because I just love taking all the monster cocks I can. They think I'm the cutest."

"That's very sweet," Erick said. "Do they care about your pleasure at all?"

Quinn closed his eyes. "Some of them do, yeah. They want to make me feel good while they fuck me."

Erick had always been a little baffled by Quinn's peculiar affinity for monsters, but he understood that once a sexual fixation took hold, it was difficult to shake, and anyway, Quinn's desires were so far into the realm of unachievable fantasy, Erick could not bring himself to see them as harmful.

"I have another one," Quinn said. "It's about both of us."

"Go ahead."

"Okay, but you have to fuck me some more."

Quinn himself might have been a mess to behold, splayed and

flushed, but Erick was trying to keep a lid on his own intense arousal. His pulse was racing, he felt uncomfortably hot all over, and his skin was damp with sweat beneath his clothes. His mind was becoming increasingly foggy as his prick got harder and harder – it was becoming a much greater effort to concentrate on giving Quinn exactly what he wanted.

"I apologize," said Erick. "Your story was very interesting, and I got distracted." He began to pump the toy in and out of Quinn again, having to listen very carefully, as Quinn's voice tended to hitch when a nice hard push gave him a full-body shudder.

"Okay, you and I are naked, and I'm on top of you, straddling you. We're just making out and rubbing against each other, and our legs are spread wide open, which makes us very vulnerable, but we think we're alone. And then a huge monster appears. Like, really huge. He's blind, and he gets most of his sensory information with his tongue." Quinn was touching himself again, relishing his own story. "So he wants to know what we are, so he starts licking us. His tongue is so big, he can lick my cock and my balls and my hole, and your cock and your balls and your hole, all at once. And he's very curious, so he licks us for like, a while, long enough that we come three times, until we're just, *ah*, just coming dry." Quinn paused, seeming to lose his train of thought, and when he continued, he was gasping and grunting. "And we're just holding each other...because we feel so *gooood*, we feel so good, but we're so scared...of how much the monster is going to make us come."

By this point, Quinn had exhausted his ability to speak coherently. His mouth hung delectably open, reduced to guttural moans by Erick's efforts. Erick's own jaw dropped as he realized how easily Quinn's hole was now taking the entire length of the toy, over and over.

Desperately craving more, Quinn lifted his legs in the air, jerking himself frantically. "*Fffuck* yeah," he growled, "fuck me with that monster cock."

Erick drove it in, while he listened to Quinn's deep grunts of pleasure. The wet sounds of too much lube made Erick's stomach flip. But then suddenly, Quinn's hand shot out and grabbed Erick's sleeve.

"Wait! I don't wanna come yet," he panted. "I don't wanna come yet."

Erick froze. "Should I take it out?"

"Uh-huh."

Erick obeyed, and as he withdrew it, Quinn groaned at the loss. "That one makes me come so hard," he said dreamily.

"I'm sure it does, my darling," Erick said, and leaned down to give Quinn a kiss on his sweaty forehead. "Tell me when you want the next one."

"Now. I don't wanna feel empty right now."

The fourth dildo was probably the most ridiculous one: a sparkly purple tentacle, which twisted dramatically. "It's a little *too* curvy," Quinn admitted. "I should have gotten the one that was more cone-shaped. If I'm not careful, this one feels poky inside. But I like the *idea* of it. And I like how the suckers tickle my hole when it goes in." He instructed Erick, with a few gestures. "Don't twist it, just put it in and wiggle it a little."

"Understood."

In fact, once he got it in, Erick barely had to move it at all; Quinn did most of the wiggling himself, cooing at the new strangeness he felt inside him.

Things had cooled off considerably, since Erick was being much gentler with this toy. Quinn said, "I have another fantasy. This one's weirder, though."

Erick smirked at that warning, delivered at *this* particular moment. "That's fine, go ahead."

"We've been captured by a monster with a huge cock. I mean, just its cock is like two or three feet long. So what we have to do to please him is, we cover our naked bodies in oil, and we sit on either side of him, and we just rub our whole bodies against his cock. We wrap our arms around each other, with his cock between us, and we can kiss each other and stuff, too. He doesn't mind, as long as we're rubbing his cock."

Quinn was right. That one *was* weirder. "Good lord," Erick said, "what happens when a monster that size ejaculates?"

"It's, uh, pretty messy," Quinn admitted. "Okay, I've had enough of the tentacle. Let's do the big one."

Though it was of a beastly size, and boasted a massive knot, the last toy had a fairly straightforward glans and shaft. Erick figured he'd just start putting it in, like he had the others, and worry about the biggest part when they came to it.

Nonetheless, he was having some trouble maintaining control, as copious amounts of lube were *everywhere*, and with his hands shaking like they were, he could hardly keep a grip on the toy as he maneuvered it. He could not believe, as he pushed this one in, that Quinn was still capable of speech, but then again, he was probably a fool to think that Quinn could ever really shut up, even if he did have a colossal dildo crammed against his prostate.

"I've got another one," was what Quinn said, while the shaft of the toy strained his already-taut rim. "This one's just me, though."

"Alright."

"There's these monsters, and in their culture it's considered honorable to have a huge cock." Quinn's thighs tensed at the pressure, but he struggled through it. "But, so, this one monster, he grows up, and his isn't very big. I mean by their standards. To us, he would still be really big. But he's cast out, and he's all alone, and I meet him, and I show him that, uh, just because his people don't think he has a big one, that's okay, because to humans, he's, uh, really big, and we like it."

"Hm, I see."

"...And the monster's name is Erick."

Erick snorted. "Oh, *stop*."

"Okay, I want the knot now."

"Are you sure you haven't had enough yet?"

"I want it really bad," Quinn insisted.

Erick suspected, however, that Quinn was not as capable as he thought he was. He grunted with the effort, as Erick struggled to give him what he begged for so greedily; his body was reluctant to allow the knot inside. "Keep pushing," he cried. "Make me take it."

"I don't want you to get hurt."

"You won't hurt me, I promise. *Hmmfh*, yeah, it's...*ohhh* fuck it's stretching me."

"I can see that."

At last, Erick watched Quinn's body give way, his rim squeezing over and around the immense knot. Quinn gasped and his spine flexed as the toy settled in at an unprecedented depth.

Erick was ready to collapse. "There you go, my darling, how's that?"

"It's nice, *oh*." Quinn tried reached down, to feel where he was more stretched and full than he ever had been before, but shifting made the dildo move inside him in a paralyzingly pleasurable way, and he collapsed back onto the mattress.

"When I tell you," Quinn said breathlessly, "I want you to slowly pull just the knot part out. I want to feel it come out when I'm coming." He started to stroke himself.

Erick put his hand back on the base of the toy, watching Quinn jerking his cock hard, squeezing the glans, straining for an orgasm. He'd never heard such harsh, dirty grunts coming from Quinn before. It was astonishingly erotic, and Erick swore with each second that passed that he would lose his mind with the intensity of his arousal.

At last, Quinn commanded, "Now!" He shouted with relief as he finally began to come, but as Erick withdrew the toy, he howled in earnest with the strain of clenching involuntarily around the knot at its thickest point. Even when the knot popped out, Quinn was still shooting spunk over his belly, so Erick continued to fuck Quinn with the toy a little bit, even through the aftershocks, watching the jolts of pleasure wrack his body.

Erick relented when Quinn lay still, but even then, Quinn said hoarsely, "Don't stop, I think I'm still coming a little bit." Erick nudged the toy once more, and Quinn groaned as his cock drooled one final little spurt.

Erick eased the toy out, watching Quinn's sore rim clinging to it. Quinn stared blankly at the ceiling as he got his breath back. After setting the toy aside, Erick sat still next to him, not wanting to disturb Quinn's recovery. But then, Quinn's head lolled to one side, and he ran his hand up and down his sticky chest and belly. He said to Erick, "Listen, um, taking all those monster dicks makes me feel kinda slutty." He rolled onto his belly, then hoisted himself up on his knees and elbows and crawled backwards to the edge of the bed. "I think I maybe need *one* more dick before I can really be satisfied...?"

Erick did not need to be told twice. He rose from the bed and got behind Quinn, gripping the behind that was being so shamelessly presented to him with one hand as he unzipped his trousers with the other. He adjusted his underwear, and his achingly hard prick tumbled out into the open air. Quinn's hole was already so open and slick with lube, Erick needed only to tilt forward, and he just slid right in; he felt filthy with how easy it was.

Knowing he would not last long anyway, Erick put his back into it, pounding Quinn with hard, rolling thrusts.

"Erick," Quinn whined sweetly, "I love your cock best of all."

That was good, Erick wanted some dirty talk to help push him over the edge. "Oh, yes?" he prompted Quinn. "Does mine make you feel slutty, too?"

Quinn went from bracing himself on his elbows up onto his hands, then pushed himself properly upright, so that his back was pressed to Erick's front. "*Nooo,*" he protested. He reached behind him to grab Erick's hands with his own, and ran them up and down his chest and belly, reveling in Erick's touch. "Yours makes me feel *loved*."

"Oh, my darling." Erick wrapped his arms tightly around Quinn as his knees were weakened by the shattering orgasm that Quinn's sweet words had prompted. He bit into the meat of Quinn's shoulder where it met his neck, so carried away was he by the intensity of this culmination.

As the blissful oblivion faded, every muscle in his body gave out entirely; he felt a little ashamed that Quinn had to help him to lie down on the bed afterwards, as he was the one who was supposed to be servicing Quinn this evening. But Quinn did not seem to mind. Not that he did a whole lot of work; once he got Erick safely and comfortably horizontal, he ran out of energy himself, leaving Erick fully dressed with his soft cock still peeking obscenely out of his trousers. They held each other, every exhalation a sigh, breathing in the strong smell of semen and lubricant which pervaded the room.

"You did it so good," Quinn said. "That was the most fun I ever had."

"It *was* a lot of fun," Erick agreed.

And then, after a long pause, he asked Quinn, "Do you think that maybe I could try that little one sometime?"

AND THEN THERE WAS THE ONE ABOUT...

THE HELPFUL BOTANIST

WITH ONE GENTLY CURLING TENTACLE, Flurr grasped at the sapling and plucked it from the damp soil. He exercised great care as he placed it in the specimen container, next to three others. Flurr had been assigned to collect seedlings and saplings in this area, and he had a limited time in which to do it, because even in the remote places that his crew limited themselves to, the ship was only to visit Earth during the darkest hours of night, when the humans were mostly asleep.

Flurr used his tentacles to brush aside ferns and low branches, looking for more specimens. Sometimes he would discover an animal instead, and those were interesting too, although nothing was as interesting as plants, if you asked him.

Flurr paused when he heard something behind him, crashing through the forest with a gait unlike any he'd heard before. This was no deer or bear. He looked in the direction of the noise, and then a bright beam of light pierced his vision. Flurr saw perfectly well in the dark, but this creature obviously couldn't, and so was using a light tool to find his way.

But if it was a tool-using creature, on Earth, that almost certainly meant it was a human! Flurr's superiors had warned him that he should under no circumstances make contact with those. But he was frozen with fear, and deep down he was a little curious, too. Surely it couldn't hurt if he just said hello to one human, one time.

When the human shone the light directly on Flurr, it immediately began to form loud, sharp words.

"Don't hurt me!" Flurr said, covering his face with his tentacles, to shield himself from the harsh light. "I'm just collecting plants!"

The human stepped slowly but loudly closer, shining the light up and down Flurr's body. "Holy shit, are you an alien?"

"I suppose I am...?" Flurr relaxed a little. "Specifically, though, I'm Flurr."

"I'm Troy," the human said. "But for serious: are you a real alien? Or is this one of the guys pulling a prank?"

"Who are the guys?"

"The guys, the ones I'm out here camping with." Troy took big steps over fallen branches to get right up close to Flurr and examine him. Flurr felt self-conscious when he noticed that Troy was staring in particular at his slick and gently swaying tentacles.

"Listen, man," Troy said, "I just wandered out here a little ways because me and my buddies are sharing a tent, and I kinda needed to jerk off." He seemed hypnotized by the perfectly ordinary movements of Flurr's tentacles as they undulated and contracted. "And, uh, I'm tripping balls right now, so I'm not sure this is really happening, but do you like, want to maybe help me out a little?"

This human seemed calmer now that they had been introduced. And Flurr *did* want to be helpful. "Only if you don't tell anyone," he said. "I'm not supposed to talk to humans."

"Dude, no one would believe me even if I did tell them." Troy began to take his clothes off. "I'm not gonna lie, those tentacles are giving me some naughty thoughts. You think you could slip one in me? I mean, since we're keeping secrets."

Flurr looked at his perfectly ordinary tentacles. He supposed it was understandable that a human might be interested in them, not having any themselves. "I could, yes. Just tell me what to do."

Troy turned his back to Flurr and braced himself against a tree. He stuck out his rear end, then reached back with one hand to pull his cheeks apart, exposing a tiny pink orifice. "Can you just slide one of those tentacles in there a little ways while I jerk it?"

Flurr had no idea what the point of doing that was, but it wasn't any trouble, so he didn't refuse. He tentatively touched the tip of a tentacle to the little pucker.

One of Troy's hands started working rhythmically on something in front of him. "Unh, yeah, put that bad boy right up there." He laughed, seemingly at his own words. "Sorry, but something about getting high makes me want to put things in my ass. I guess I get like, disinhabited. Disinhibited."

The little orifice was tight, but it stretched to accommodate Flurr's tentacle. "Push it in," Troy demanded. "Fuck, that's deep, that's so deep." Flurr kept going, until Troy said, "Stop. That's good, my dude, that's enough."

Flurr held still for a while, until Troy said, "Okay, now you can pull it out a little."

Flurr obeyed, withdrawing, but once he had, Troy said, "Now push it back in." And he kept on like that: "Pull it out. Push it in. Pull it out."

"I don't mean to be rude," Flurr said, "but could you make up your mind? I have to collect thirty-six more plants tonight."

"Just keep doing it a little more. Oh. Oh. *Ohhh*, yeah. Fuck, yeah." Troy's hand moved very fast for a moment, then stopped. He heaved a huge sigh, and his legs shook. "Okay, okay, you can take it out now. That felt amazing. Shit, the guys are gonna wonder where I am."

Troy tried to get himself back into his clothes, but when he did, Flurr noticed that his shirt was oriented differently than it had been before. Troy asked, "Do you happen to remember what direction I came from?"

Flurr pointed.

"Thanks. Hey listen, alien buddy, I like you. Look me up any time you're in town."

Troy wandered back into the woods, even more unsteadily than when he'd arrived.

Flurr was sad that he would not be able to tell any of his

colleagues about meeting a human. But he consoled himself by imagining that one day, if his people ever decided that the time had come to formally introduce themselves to the planet Earth, he could confide in detail to the chosen ambassadors his insider knowledge of exactly how humans greeted each other.

THE WILDERNESS BEYOND

As the flyer made its way to Mason Winter's module, Tobias reviewed his notes, and had another look at an article written by another journalist about Mason's home. Mason had recently become a noteworthy personality after having been assigned a module – it was the same as everyone else's module on the colony, but Mason had distinguished himself by making it into a *home*, a real, comfy, cozy home. Tobias gazed with not a little envy at the pictures in the article, observing the meticulous planning, collecting, and decorating that must have gone into turning a sterile, nearly-featureless module into a residence that one would look at admiringly and feel good being in.

Tobias had his own resourcefulness, however, which had gotten him an invitation to meet with Mason. Since that first article about Mason had been published, other journalists had clamored for a glimpse into his lifestyle, a chance to write about how he had brought comfort, style, and perhaps even just a little bit of glamour into an otherwise utilitarian colony. Tobias had been one of the very few people Mason had said "yes" to; he had asked to interview Mason about his eating habits and cooking skills, a specific aspect of his lifestyle that had been glossed over in the other article in favor of examining the fine details of his upholstered furniture and elegant hand-sewn curtains.

The flyer dropped Tobias at the edge of the neighborhood, and he navigated the grid of walkways until he found what was unmistakably Mason's home: according to the article Tobias had been re-reading, the paint was ground-up plant matter, and the elaborate but symmetrical decorations on the door were repurposed scraps that he had scavenged.

Mason answered the door promptly and cheerfully when Tobias knocked. His appearance was warmer, a little more casual, than the pictures that had accompanied the article, which had shown him well-groomed but awkwardly posed next to the most aesthetically-pleasing of his possessions. There was a timelessness about his personal style, but at the same time, a quirkiness in the fine details – the patterns of the fabric, the width of the sleeves, the length of his hair. This was a man who was definitely making an enormous personal effort to be "eccentric" in a place where conformity was not enforced by law but was almost universal because it was just so much *easier*.

"Thank you so much for taking the time to speak to me," Tobias said, as Mason invited him inside.

"It's my pleasure. I've read some of your writing, and it seems that you, like me, are very interested in improving the quality of colony life."

"Well, my job isn't *officially* Public Relations for the Colonial Division, but that's what it usually comes down to. Just you allowing me to interview you is honestly invaluable to us; polls taken back on Earth have consistently revealed that people are less willing to live on one of the off-world settlements mainly because they think it's boring and ugly, and food is a huge factor in that. Most people don't want to eat protein cubes, and the few who don't have a problem with it are already here. If I can show the people back on Earth that it's possible to eat tasty, nutritious meals here, well, I guess you'll have a whole lot more neighbors."

"A delightful prospect. Excuse me for just a moment, I've just got to grab something." Mason went into the other room, while Tobias decided that the dining table he was standing next to was as good a place as any to settle in.

"Would you like to do the interview here?" Tobias called out. He took out his recorder and his stylus, and set them on the table. Mason returned then, carrying something, the handle of it over the crook of his arm. It was not a carry-pod but a basket, an actual basket, no doubt hand-woven by Mason himself.

"The weather is mild today," Mason said, "and I thought that perhaps instead of just talking about the foods I cook with, you might like to help me harvest them, and if you haven't anywhere to be this evening, we can cook them together."

This was unexpected. "Wow, that would be fantastic," Tobias said.

"I suppose I've become famous for my eminently habitable habitation, but in my opinion, having a little exercise outdoors is always better than staying cooped up inside a house of any sort. Have you ever been outside the city?"

Tobias shook his head. "Work has kept me busy since I was stationed here. I've heard the wilderness beyond the colony is beautiful, though."

Moments after they stepped outside the module, a flyer descended; Mason must have ordered it before Tobias's arrival, so confident was he in Tobias's agreement to this outing.

"How much of an adventure will this be, exactly?" Tobias asked, gazing out the window as the flyer rose again and headed for the untamed outskirts of the settlement.

"Oh, nothing too exciting. At the edge of the city is a patch of jungle that has not yet been touched by any clumsy terraforming efforts. A delicious fruit grows there, called the yuafflon. Its delicate sweetness makes it perfect for compotes, and I require several of them for a dinner party I am hosting the day after tomorrow. But we can set aside a little for ourselves." At this, he smiled at Tobias, like they were sharing a secret.

With a furrowed brow, Tobias asked, "Is it dangerous? I mean, you called it a 'jungle.' Is it like jungles on Earth, where everything tried to kill you?"

"Oh, it's not nearly as exciting as that," Mason said. "We'll be perfectly safe."

Having reached the far edge of the settlement, the flyer descended. Mason examined the total charge on the screen, found it satisfactory, and touched his card to the screen to debit his account. "We have a little more walking to do, before we reach the grove where the yuafflon grow."

"That's fine." Tobias inhaled deeply. They were close enough to the wilderness that the air quality was already distinctly different; richer, full of the untidy and chaotic smells of nature. Mason led the way past the low ferns and vines that threatened to erode the settlement's fringes, and into the thick of the forest, which was free of trails or markers.

"I'm assuming you know the way," Tobias said, more of a statement than an inquiry.

"My sense of direction is excellent. I assure you we will not get lost." Mason adjusted the basket on his arm, lifting it occasionally to keep it free of grasping vines.

Tobias had no idea what the yuafflon looked like; Mason had not given him a clue about what to look for. So he allowed himself to take in the sights indiscriminately: the massively thick overhanging leaves and the sunlight that broke through them to reflect off of opalescent puddles; the sprays of branches in flower and the buzzing fist-sized insects that traveled from one to another. The only guidance Mason gave him was to mutter, "Don't get too close to those," when Tobias wandered past a vine that reached for him with stunning precision.

"I heard there's a new farmer's market being set up by the council," Tobias said. "Can you not just buy some yuafflon there?"

"Unfortunately, no. The yuafflon is supported by acres of roots. It's not feasible to domesticate it in such a small settlement. And harvesting large quantities from the jungle is not yet sufficiently cost-effective to make it an attractive commodity. Ah, here we are."

Mason stopped before a little cluster of elongated fruits, each of them just a few inches long and only a shade darker than the leaves that surrounded them.

"These are not quite ripe enough, but there should be more nearby. They turn a deep red when they're ripe."

"I'll keep an eye out," Tobias said. He stayed close to Mason, his gaze a little higher now that he knew they grew at eye level. Scanning the area, he saw another cluster of fruit, similarly shaped but larger and red, about twenty yards off. "Over here," he said, and tramped off in that direction.

As he approached the yuafflon, he caught sight of something else: a much larger fruit, hanging off a thicker vine, which intertwined somewhat with the yuafflon plant. Each specimen was ovoid, and easily more than two handfuls, a bright blue where it attached to the vine, fading to purple toward the opposite end. Tobias could detect a luscious odor rising from the fruit, and he suddenly remembered that he hadn't had much for breakfast. "Hey, are these any good to eat, do you know?"

Mason did not answer, and Tobias turned around to find that he was not there. He was not in sight. Tobias called out, but got no response. This should have been much more worrying than it was, but Tobias could not help but return his attention to his strange new discovery. Even just the color of it was oddly fascinating; one could hardly perceive the transition from blue to purple, it was so smooth. Tobias got closer, to have a better look, and was overwhelmed by the intoxicating odor. Nothing that smelled that good could possibly be poisonous. No lethal plant would give off an *enticing* odor...would it?

Tobias reached out to pluck one of the fruits from the vine. He hardly needed to pull; the moment he touched it, it seemed to just fall right into his waiting hands. He hefted it, found it quite solid, but when he pressed with both thumbs, it burst open, like it had been waiting for him to do so. The scent was much stronger now, and the sticky pulp slicked his hands.

Suddenly Tobias felt his stomach drop, a familiar pang that was the first flickering intimation of arousal. Within seconds, he was rendered so light-headed by this feeling, he could not even be bothered to ponder how bizarre it was that he was feeling it at all. His skin tingled, his balls ached, and his cock was painfully hard. The only thought he could process was that he needed relief, *now*.

Tobias dropped one of the halves of the fruit so that he could unzip his trousers, freeing his cock to the open air, which seemed to have grown more humid in the last several seconds. Doing this made him marginally more comfortable, but he was still suffering from a congestion in his genitals the likes of which he had never experienced before.

Mason would know what to do about this. He would help. But Tobias made a full turn, and Mason was still nowhere to be seen. Each exhalation was a whimper now, as Tobias looked down at his left hand, which held the other half of the fruit. It was dark purple, rich and wet inside. He pressed a finger to it, found it gooey and yielding. Tobias was so far gone, so consumed with lust, he did not for an instant consider the possible consequences. He pressed the fruit against himself, sank his throbbing cock into it, all the way, until his pubic hair was matted with the dark pulp. He viciously fucked the soft, sloppy meat of the fruit, seeking the quickest possible conclusion, lured by the dim promise of relief from the agony of his lust. But even as his orgasm crept up, he could feel that it would not be enough. He chased it anyway, shouting with continued frustration, as the moment of ecstasy provided no respite. His cock remained hard, and pulsed with even greater intensity. Weakened and despondent, Tobias fell to his knees on the forest floor, sinking slightly into the thick carpet of moss. That was how Mason found him.

As far as Mason was concerned, there was little need to ask what had happened. Any explanation that Tobias might be able to eke out would likely prove less clear than the sight before him. And so he made only the most pertinent inquiry: "When did you find yourself overcome? When you smelled it? When you ate it?"

"No, I didn't eat it," Tobias said, his voice strained and creaking, "I just touched the pulp with my hands."

Dermal transmission. That was helpful to know.

"Please," Tobias panted, delirious. "Fuck me. I need it. I need it so bad."

"Do you think the feeling will subside if I do that?"

"I think so. Maybe. Please, just do *something*."

Mason took a moment to consider the best approach. He found Tobias physically attractive, and was utterly unopposed to the idea of sex with him, though he had not anticipated that this adventure would result in sex, and so he had not brought a suitable lubricant. There was only the sopping guts of the fruit, and he dared not touch that; if he was certain of one thing, it was that he would be of greater assistance to Tobias if he himself did not fall victim to the fruit's intoxicating effects.

His eyes fell upon the basket, which he'd dropped when he'd found Tobias incapacitated, and he realized he had a solution. The yuafflon. Cylindrical, elongated, and slightly tapered at one end. It would suffice. Mason took a yuafflon from the basket and, careful not to get any on his bare hands, dug the narrower end into the pulp of the half of the fruit that Tobias had dropped.

"Lean forward, on your elbows," he instructed, and Tobias immediately complied. With his trousers already pulled down, his bare ass was in the air and easily accessible.

"I will endeavor not to hurt you," Mason said, and pushed the slickened end of the yuafflon into Tobias's hole.

"Oh God, fucking yeah, that's what I need." Ravenous, Tobias pushed back onto the yuafflon, prompting Mason to hiss a warning. He had to keep his grip firm and his hand steady, watching to make sure the makeshift lubricant did not reach his fingers, even as it gathered around Tobias's rim and along the shaft of the yuafflon.

"*Ungh*, fuck me with it," Tobias hollered, and Mason honored his request, twisting the yuafflon inside him, trying to find the angle that was the most gratifying. When he had managed to arrange it so that the curve of it rubbed consistently against Tobias's prostate, he proceeded with a relentless rhythm.

"Yes, fuck yes, this is...this is gonna do it, I can feel it.

Can...fff...yeah..." Tobias said something else, but he was laboring for breath and had become incoherent. He uttered a thick, prolonged grunt as he tugged at his sore, stiff prick, ejaculating hard but thinly into the lush moss beneath him.

Mason's grip on the yuafflon was so tight, when Tobias's thighs trembled and gave out, he slipped right off of it as he crumpled to the forest floor, leaving Mason holding the fruit incongruously in mid-air. He set it aside and observed Tobias, who appeared sated, and approaching a state of calm.

"What the hell just happened," Tobias murmured. "What the hell just..."

"I think it might be a good idea to leave this little grove now, before either of us inadvertently finds ourselves in contact with more of that fruit. Can you get up by yourself? I fear I might touch a stray bit of pulp if I try to lift you bodily."

"I can do it." Tobias got his arms and legs under him, and pushed himself up, groaning all the while. It was only when he got to his feet that he seemed to realize that his trousers were still undone and around his thighs. Mortified, he hastily got himself arranged. "I'm so sorry, this is a hell of a way to make a first impression on someone."

"Don't trouble yourself," Mason said lightly as he picked up the basket of yuafflon. "You succumbed to a nasty mind-altering substance in unfamiliar territory. It does not reflect on you as a person, and I don't feel there's any need to mention this incident in your article. Well, so, back to civilization, then, hm?"

Mason pointed the way, let Tobias get in front of him, and then carefully – oh so carefully – plucked one of the strange new fruits from its vine, concealing it beneath the yuafflon in his basket.

THE FUTURESIGHT BLUES

There was a long moment of relative quiet, while all non-essential systems throughout the entire wing were shut down. Adrian Grahame stood stock-still next to Vik Anand while they waited for the activation sequence to commence. "Don't lock your knees," Vik muttered to Adrian. "You don't want to pass out again like you did at the Amulite demonstration."

Adrian bent his knees a little, though nothing else was being done to actually relieve his tension in any meaningful way, and so seconds later, he had locked them again. What he really would have liked to have done was hold Vik's hand, but that, he felt, would require a long conversation first, during which he would reveal his feelings to his closest friend and colleague, and explain why he thought they would make a good match outside of the lab as well as being effective partners within it. He had put that imaginary conversation off for too long, however, not even sure at this point that Vik knew that Adrian considered him his closest friend. They might need to have *two* conversations. But for right now, it was too late; the activation of the viewing device was mere moments away.

The project lead, Konstatin Schweiger, gave the first order. "Initiate inverse reactive current," he said, and with a curt nod, engineer Jeanne Kopp opened up the unilateral phase detractors. A new, sharp kind of hum filled the room, lower and harsher than the usual ambient buzzing of fluorescent lights, CPUs, and the HVAC system. Adrian sweated while he waited for his instruction.

"Synchronize cardinal grammeters," Dr. Schweiger said, and Adrian watched Vik manipulate the odeltoid-type semi-boloid slots. He always found the sight of Vik working with his hands riveting, but this time he was so distracted he nearly forgot that what he really ought to be looking at was in front of him: the viewscreen, ten feet high and until this moment dark. Now, it slowly grew brighter, though it showed nothing but grayish noise.

Dr. Schweiger said, "Increase modial interaction of magneto-reluctance." This was Adrian's cue. He rotated the ambiphasient wainshaft, and the differential girdle-spring began its phorescent motion. After doing this he looked up again. Could he detect a pattern on the screen now? Surely it must be his imagination. The capacitive chronometric vanes had not even been engaged yet.

But then the screen began to flash wildly, the overhead lights flickered, and the noise from the girdle-spring was unlike anything they had heard during any of the dry-runs of the activation sequence. "Reduce the sonosoidal retuperation!" shouted Dr. Schweiger, and Adrian struggled with the drawn reciprocation arm. But once he had overcome the resistance, the chilling sound from the girdle-spring vanished, the lights glowed steadily again, and the screen...

An image had appeared on the screen.

The image was new, but familiar, strange, but comprehensible. It was a city – their city. Jeanne recognized the iconic Tremi Building, and pointed it out. On the screen, it was dwarfed on all sides by glittering towers, and all around this cluster of skyscrapers, flying transports of varying shapes flitted about.

"Congratulations, team" Dr. Schweiger announced, "Thanks to your years of patient effort, we are looking one hundred years into the future."

Awed beyond reason, Adrian suddenly stopped caring about decorum or proper timing, and grasped Vik's hand. They were behind the grammeters, so no one else could see. When Vik squeezed Adrian's hand back, Adrian nearly fell over – the idea that his feelings might be reciprocated was nearly as much of a revelation as what was currently being shown on the time-viewer.

"Look at how blue the sky is," Vik said. "And off in the distance – some sort of reforestation effort?"

"Beautiful," was all Adrian could get to come out of his mouth. He didn't have the capacity at the moment to articulate his relief at seeing that in one hundred years, Earth, or at least this sliver of it, would be lovelier and more habitable than their current circumstances.

There was some concern that keeping the viewing window open for too long might cause a space-time disturbance, and so by Dr. Schweiger's orders, the screen went blank after a mere sixty seconds. But immediately afterwards, a recording of that minute of the future city was passed along to the relevant analysts, and the activation team were instructed to write and file their reports.

Adrian kept close to Vik, and when the rest of the team filed out in front of them, he tapped Vik on the shoulder and asked him if he would stay behind for a moment.

"We can talk here, if you like," Vik said. "But the closed-circuit cameras are still operating here, so we might want to go somewhere with no prying eyes...my quarters, perhaps?"

Adrian blushed. "Oh, well," he stammered, "if you're amenable."

Even though all the various speeches that Adrian had practiced – that he had tailored for different circumstances and refined over the years – soon proved to have been a waste of time and effort, he could not bring himself to be sad about it. The moment Vik's door was closed and they looked each other in the eye, it became clear that every necessary word had already been said, every preliminary act had already been carried out, in all the laboratories they had shared over the years, all the libraries and corridors and cafeterias.

There had followed a few frantic kisses, a little groping, and now they were making their way to a bed – Adrian had directed them there, because under the circumstances it seemed to be the most appropriate place for what they were doing, more appropriate than the desk had been. If they'd had access to a sofa, he might have chosen that as their venue. He was nervous about what they were doing, unsure of how far they would go, and while a sofa could technically be used for every imaginable act, there was also a feeling of limitation attached to it: you could just make out on a sofa, and that would be fine. Being on the bed, as they now were, it felt like merely making out might not be...sufficient?

In any event, they were at each other like teenagers, still fully clothed. Or so Adrian guessed; he had not actually experienced anything like this when he was a teenager. But he imagined that this was what it would have been like.

He studiously followed Vik's lead: when Vik yanked Adrian's sweater and shirt up and stuck his hand underneath, Adrian's fingers scrabbled at the hem of Vik's shirt to get it untucked from his jeans. When Vik gasped or groaned, he allowed himself to utter similar sounds.

But as they went on, he found that he was having a difficult time focusing on what he should be doing to Vik, so consumed was he by the novelty of being touched by someone else's hands and mouth. To be grabbed, caressed, pinched, felt, and gripped was alien to him, as was the very idea that his merely existing might be enough to satisfy another's desires.

And there were sex noises – the sounds of moist mucous membranes sliding against each other. It was just a press of mouths, but when he heard them, he felt something hot and shivery engulfing his entire body, his insides, his whole being. Vik was licking inside his mouth, and that seemed so ridiculous, but every swipe of his tongue sent shocks of pleasure through him.

He was sweating, hot and damp all over. He wanted to stop and take his clothes off, but that would mean not kissing for several seconds, taking his mouth away from Vik's to get his sweater off over his head, taking his concentration from Vik's skin to focus instead on vexing buttons. He simply could not force himself to divert from his course.

As they panted hotly into each other's mouths, Vik's hand slipped out from under Adrian's shirt to slide down, over the fabric of his trousers, between his legs, and Adrian gasped as his vision whited out and he was wracked by searing pulses of pleasure. His eyes rolled back and his body convulsed. Then, by chance, he made eye contact with Vik again, and held it while several more little shudders rippled through his body. Then he blinked, looked down at himself, and whined softly with the most intense mortification he had ever felt – which was a high bar.

"Oh my God," Vik said, "did you just come?"

Adrian cringed. "I, ah...yes."

Vik, however, smiled fondly at this admission. "So it was good, then?"

"What?" The question shook Adrian from his humiliation, just for a moment, just long enough to be baffled.

"Did it feel good?"

Adrian opened his mouth as if to reply, but said nothing. He was bright red, hot with embarrassment from his neck to his ears. Vik he grabbed Adrian's hand and laid the palm flat against the ridge that throbbed beneath his own zipper. "Here, I'll do it too. Just put your hand on me. It's okay, kiss me, just rub it and kiss me."

Adrian opened his mouth to kiss Vik ferociously as he slid his palm up and down, learning the shape of Vik's erection, pressing hard to feel its little twitches when Vik cried out into his mouth. Vik clutched and tugged at Adrian's sweater with both hands as he came, and it was so wonderful to feel that wildness between them, Adrian hardly knew what to do. He waited for further guidance, while Vik slumped into a content lethargy.

"There, do you feel better that I did it too?" Vik said dreamily.

"A little. But also not, because...it's over." Adrian looked down at the damp patches on their trousers, honestly not certain if he was still embarrassed.

"Nothing's over. If you want, we can get naked and get under the covers and cuddle, now. And then, you know. How long is it gonna take you to be ready for round two?"

Adrian blinked. "I've no idea. I've never...timed myself."

"Really? Is it just me that does that?" Vik went to work on shirt and trouser buttons, his own and Adrian's, releasing them both from their sweaty, confining clothes, while Adrian mostly sat in a daze. Throwing back the covers, Vik crawled into bed and, still holding the blanket up, invited Adrian to join him.

Adrian's eyes traveled down Vik's body. He had sort of seen Vik naked once, when a lab accident had necessitated an emergency shower for both of them. But he had politely averted his eyes, then. Now he was simply staring at Vik's penis, thinking, *I was just touching that.* A moment later, it occurred to him: *He was just touching mine, as well, kind of. What an odd afternoon this has been.*

Vik tilted his head and shook the corner of the blanket. "Come on and get in, no one's gonna miss us for just a couple hours."

Hmm. A "couple hours" under this blanket with Vik. Adrian was glad now, that they were not on a sofa.

If the first time-viewer activation was nerve-wracking, Adrian could barely keep himself still for the second run. The stress of having a crush on Vik was like nothing compared to what he was going through now; he had learned to deal with *that* over several years. The stress of wondering if everyone else on the team could tell that he and Vik had recently been intimate for the first time – that was a whole new kind of terror.

But if anyone was aware of anything unusual, they said nothing. Dr. Schweiger directed the team through the activation process once more, and this time, there was no excess of sonosoidal retuperation; the team worked smoothly to bring the view of the city, as it looked one hundred years hence, to the viewscreen.

But this view, while still unmistakably the same city, was very different. The rotting, skeletal remains of the Tremi Building and other towers were surrounded on all sides by a blighted landscape of ruins and desert, and engulfed in a brown haze.

The team stared in abject horror at the screen, shocked at how different the next century now looked, compared to the day before.

Jeanne broke the silence by suggesting, "The butterfly effect?"

Dr. Schweiger agreed. "It would appear that something happened in the last day, which drastically altered Earth's fate."

Adrian's heart leapt into his throat. Surely everyone was panicking now, but not like *he* was, for he had a very strong suspicion about what had changed.

The analysts were brought in, and Doctor Schweiger conferred with them. Adrian and Vik remained at their stations and were ignored in the commotion. Adrian sidled up to Vik and whispered, "You don't suppose this happened because we..." He gulped, and looked at the floor, embarrassed. "Because of what we did?"

Vik glanced at Adrian, then back at the screen. "It seems unlikely. I mean, a trillion things have happened all over the world since yesterday."

"But only the four of us observed it directly," Adrian said, his voice not so much a whisper as a hiss. "What if we affected the future by viewing it? If we hadn't observed it, I wouldn't have held your hand, and then we wouldn't, you know..." Adrian began to pace back and forth behind the grammeters. "Oh, what have we done? Our base impulses have destroyed civilization!"

"Adrian, calm down. The odds of us being responsible are very, very, very small."

From the other side of the room Dr. Schweiger took notice of them, and barked, "Doctor Anand, Doctor Grahame, do you have any insights to share?"

"None at all!" Adrian shrieked, and at the same time, Vik said, "Nothing of any real substance."

"Um, except," Adrian said, now that all eyes were on them, "if we're the ones who are responsible – and by 'we,' I mean the whole team, and by 'responsible, I mean observing the future, of course, I'm not making any other more specific implication – then maybe we need to shut the viewscreen off again, right now?"

"That may be best," Dr. Schweiger said, "until we have a better idea of what's going on."

The shutdown sequence was initiated, and afterwards Dr. Schweiger announced that all parties present would reconvene in the campus' main meeting room in two hours – once he could get a few quantum physicists from several different nations on a conference call. In the meantime, he dismissed the group, but warned everyone not to leave campus and to consider themselves on-call.

Adrian and Vik pretended to be going to their separate quarters, but once the others lost sight of them, they both headed for Adrian's room. There, Adrian flopped onto his bunk and fretted for half an hour or so, while Vik attempted to comfort him, and dissuade him of the notion that they were the reason for Earth's future collapse.

"It probably just seems like what we did was enough to change the world so drastically because it was so meaningful and monumental to *us*," he reasoned.

Adrian stopped his trembling in the fetal position and looked up. "It was meaningful and monumental to you?" he asked.

"Of course it was." Vik came over and sat next to Adrian on the bed, and leaned down for a kiss, but Adrian turned his head and muttered, "No, that might make things worse."

"I'm really, really sure we're not responsible."

Adrian pounded his fists on the mattress. "But how can we *know*?"

"Maybe there is a way we can know," Vik said. "Do you trust me?"

Adrian nodded.

"Then come with me."

The lab was deserted, but Adrian reminded Vik that everyone would know they were making an unauthorized entry – even if they somehow turned the closed-circuit cameras off, they were using their own biometric information to enter. "Then I'll guess we'll just have to ask really hard for forgiveness," Vik said. "Now, we'll have to do a little running back and forth to do the activation sequence by ourselves."

"We're going to turn the viewscreen on again?"

"What did you think we were coming in here to do? And anyway, you said you trusted me."

"I do."

"So go stand by the grammeters."

This time when the viewscreen was activated, Adrian and Vik once again saw a different city: crystalline structures draped in brilliant green flora, like the Hanging Gardens of Babylon. The entire sprawling metropolis, in fact, appeared to be a veritable ecotopia, with nature seamlessly integrated into a pristine urban infrastructure.

"Oh, well now that looks nice," Adrian mused.

"Let's do it again."

They toiled through the shutdown sequence, then the activation sequence again, and this time, the viewscreen showed a barren tundra, with not even the ruins of any buildings in sight. This did not help Adrian's anxiety, but Vik insisted, "If we look again, it will be different again. And the next time. And you and I have not fooled around in the last few minutes, as far as I'm aware."

Adrian had to concede this point. He and Vik shut the screen down again, and Vik took Adrian's hands in his own and said, "We can't be certain about what's on the screen or why it's on the screen. But what I'm certain of is, whatever the future brings, I want to share it with you. Now, we've got to go, or we're going to be late for that conference call."

The video call included four of the greatest minds in physics, each of whom felt that they were *the* greatest mind, and made themselves the center of attention accordingly. Dr. Schweiger attempted to moderate them, to synthesize their ideas about what the images on the viewscreen meant, but he finally had to mute them all, and then turned back to the room. "I'd be interested to hear what opinions any of you might have," he said. "Especially you, Doctors Anand and Grahame."

Adrian had *known* they'd be immediately found out. He was so ashamed, he wished that Dr. Schweiger would have chosen to instead push a button that would cause his chair to be dropped into a tank full of ravenous sharks, so he would suffer less than he was suffering right then. Next to him, Vik leaned forward, rested his elbows on the table, and said, "As a matter of fact, we have put some work into this, and we believe there are two possibilities: first, that there is only one world, and one future, but the future is constantly in flux, and thus impossible to know until we view it and collapse the waveform. The second possibility is that there are many worlds, and each time we activate the viewscreen, we are viewing one of these many existing futures. Therefore, we believe it is not *inherently* harmful to view the future. I do believe that we need to start considering the ethical implications of anyone at all, including ourselves, having access to information about the future, particularly once we can refine the machine to look at times nearer to us than one hundred years, and more closely than a distant cityscape."

"Alright," said Schweiger, "we are tentatively allowing further activation of the viewscreen for the analysts to study these hypotheses." He eyed Adrian and Vik. "But *only* under my personal supervision." He gave a few more instructions, then adjourned the meeting.

Adrian stood, straight-backed and staring forward, to try to mask his panic, but once outside and out of Dr. Schweiger's view he clutched his chest and gasped, "I thought for sure we were going to be terminated."

Vik chuckled. "Surely not. Wait, do you mean terminated as in 'fired' or terminated as in 'killed'?"

Adrian shrugged. "First one, then the other?"

"Well, that's the trick to breaking the rules, isn't it?" Vik gripped Adrian's shoulder. "You can only do it if you're a super genius and you know you can come out looking like a hero."

"You knew we'd come out looking like heroes?"

"I sure didn't." He tapped his index finger against his temple. "But I had a hypothesis."

"A hypothesis about you being a super genius, or a hypothesis about the meaning of the images on the viewscreen?"

Vik shrugged, and grinned. "First one, then the other?"

AND THEN THERE WAS THE ONE ABOUT...

THE GUY WHO LOCKED HIMSELF OUT OF HIS HOUSE

PATTING his pockets down one last time, Neil cursed his absent-mindedness. This was not the first time he had forgotten his keys. He knocked on the door, but Roger did not answer, which was the case sometimes when he was upstairs.

It was a summer day, warm but breezy, and Neil walked around the house, hoping that one of the windows on the ground floor had been left open. Luckily for him, there was an open window into the dining room. Breaking in was a struggle, as he had to climb over some shrubbery and heave himself up to get in. He made such a commotion that he attracted the attention of a passing police officer on patrol. The officer got out of his hover-cruiser and ran across the yard, shouting at Neil to stop where he was.

Neil dropped back down to the ground with a sigh; he'd nearly climbed in. "This is just a misunderstanding," he said, his hands in the air. "I live here. I can show you my identification, which has this address on it."

The police officer allowed Neil to – slowly – get his identification out of his pocket. It looked to be in order, and showed that he was a resident of this house. "I would still like to walk through the house with you," the officer said, "just to make sure that nothing suspicious is happening."

"By all means," Neil shrugged, "if you can let me in."

The officer used his pass-key device, facilitated by Neil's fingerprint, to open the front door. Neil made a big show of there being nothing wrong or strange. He showed the officer into the living room, where framed pictures were crowded on the mantelpiece. "See, here's me in all these photos, with my husband Roger," he said. Then he led a tour through the kitchen and into the bathroom, where he showed the officer the prescription medications with his name on the label. "This one I take when I have stomach problems, and this one's for my insomnia." From there, Neil led the officer up the stairs and into the master bedroom. "Roger's probably up here," he said.

The door was open, and the two of them found Roger on the bed, splayed in the lap of – and being roughly and noisily plowed by – an enormous, hairy beast. The creature had to be seven feet tall, snarling and grunting with teeth bared. Its massive hands easily enveloped Roger's waist, as it moved Roger back and forth on its colossal cock, which was clearly visible to Neil and the police officer as it moved, huge and slick, in and out of Roger's asshole. Roger moaned and cooed with each thrust, his face pressed against the monster's furry chest. He clutched at its brawny middle, making every effort to keep his balance with his legs spread improbably wide as it bounced him.

The police officer stood behind Neil, watching Roger being joyously fucked for a moment or two, until Neil turned around and said, "So that's Roger, my husband." Walking back down the hall, he went on: "Anyway, thank you so much for letting me back in. If you have another few minutes, I've got a wonderful French press in the kitchen, and I can make you a cup of coffee for your trouble." At the bottom of the stairs, Neil turned and went into the kitchen, with the police officer close on his heels.

"But what about that huge monster that was fucking your husband?" the officer cried.

"Oh, him?" Neil said with a shrug, as he grabbed the tin containing the coffee grounds. "He practically lives here. He knows where the press is; he can get his own cup of coffee."

YOUR SAFETY IS IMPORTANT

DREW WAS SO NERVOUS, he flubbed his very first line.

"Good peace and fortune to you," he greeted Anvar, the aide who was to take Cade and himself to see the Minister of Technology – and he'd just talked over Cade, who at the same moment had flawlessly said the correct greeting: "Peace and good fortune to you."

In the transport tunnel, Drew burned with embarrassment. It was easy for Cade to perform perfectly; he had learned every word of the Velb dialect, including its topsy-turvy grammar, prior to their journey. He stood next to Drew now, straight-backed and dignified, carrying a heavy bag as though it were weightless; it would have been better, Drew had maintained, for Cade to have traveled to the Velb world alone, to explain and demonstrate his own features and functions. But no contract or agreement was valid if the sole representative of either side was an android, and so here Drew was, an egghead who had spent his life sequestered away in laboratories, designing, building, and perfecting androids specifically so that he would never have to learn how to be socially adept.

The transport doors opened to a spacious and sleek anteroom, where they waited to be announced. Anvar then invited them through the archway to be met by the Minister of Technology.

Taking a deep breath, Drew inclined his head slightly toward the

Minister, saying, "Peace and good fortune to you." Cade did the same, effortlessly. Then Drew remembered that there was a second nod of the head he'd forgotten, and he overcompensated for it so hard he nearly gave himself whiplash.

The Minister chuckled. "Doubtless you were given strict instructions about the draconian niceties on the Velb world."

"Indeed we were, Minster," Cade answered for them.

"Do not trouble yourself so," the Minister continued to address Drew. "We are sons of a common ancestor. You are quite welcome here."

Despite this declaration of interplanetary human brotherhood, Drew understood what the Minister really meant: *Our respective societies are in a position where trade is more beneficial than war, so we will probably not burn down your civilization for minor errors in etiquette. Probably.*

Only now did the Minister acknowledge Cade. "And this is the android."

Confirming that this was so, Drew clapped Cade on the shoulder, patting him like he was just some ordinary consumer product. "Our absolute top-of-the-line model, but already in mass production. If you like him, we can get you eight thousand each lunar cycle...with the standard interplanetary shipping delay, obviously."

"Of course. If you would come this way please." The Minister checked the time as he led Drew and Cade through another archway and down a corridor, into a room of eclectic furnishings, where Cade's abilities would be put to the test. Looking around, the Minster appeared irritated, and said, "I was expecting that my team of engineers would be here by now. I am sorry to make you wait, but please do excuse me for a moment. You are welcome to have a seat over there." The Minister indicated some utilitarian chairs, near a table that had a variety of tools and objects on it.

"This is probably also a test," Drew said, in his native tongue, when they were alone.

"Most certainly. In Velb culture it is not customary to leave one's guests alone so soon after their arrival."

"But what are they testing?" Though Drew remained tense with anticipation, now that he was in no one's company but Cade's he nonetheless felt one hundred percent better. "Do you think it's to do with you...or with *us*?"

"Best not to speculate aloud, if we are indeed being monitored remotely."

Drew nodded. But there was one thing he wanted to say, now that he had the chance. He leaned close and whispered, hoping no microphone would pick it up. "Sorry about the slapping-you-on-the-shoulder thing," he said.

"Think nothing of it," Cade said, unperturbed.

When Anvar and the Minister returned, they were accompanied by two studious men in close-fitting white coats, each carrying a tablet.

Also accompanying them was a robot. An old-fashioned metal robot. His head was square, with two transceivers on either side like ears, and two photoreceptors like big dark eyes, with a speaker beneath them, to give him a semblance of a human face. He had spindly limbs and clunky feet, though his joints were finely articulated, especially his hands. Overall, a well-maintained and endearingly anthropomorphic machine, though primitive when compared to androids like Cade.

"Ooh, new humans!" The robot seemed pleasantly taken aback for a moment, and then waved cheerily. "Hello! I'm Otto!"

"Nice to meet you, Otto," Drew said, and gave the robot the same nod of his head as he'd given to the other Velb, in case it was appropriate to do so.

"Hope you don't mind," said an engineer, "we brought one of our robots along."

"Not at all," said Drew.

Otto's gestures were open and just slightly exaggerated, making him seem charmingly enthusiastic and friendly. "I love meeting new humans!" he said. "I've met humans from Yur, Hraff, and Gunnpor. Where are you from?"

"Oh, er, my planet is called Vude," Drew said.

"Vude! I know a story about that place!"

Otto clasped his hands behind his back as he began to recite:

There once was a woman from Vude...

Drew's jaw dropped, and his blood pressure immediately skyrocketed. Otto was about to recite a limerick? This could be an amusing icebreaker...or it could be a diplomatic disaster, depending on the level of bawdiness.

Who went for a swim in the nude...

Drew cringed. The bawdiness level had just swung into the red.

A man in a punt...

It was all Drew could do to stay standing; his knees had turned to water. Was no one going to stop this robot?

Stuck his pole in the water...

Drew blinked. That definitely did not rhyme with "punt."

And said, "You can't swim here, it's private."

Never in his life had Drew been so utterly relieved. The breath he'd been holding turned to a laugh as the cleverness of Otto's poem sank in. All humans present joined him, Anvar and the engineers waiting to chuckle or guffaw until they saw the Minister do so.

Unused to Otto's antics, Drew continued to laugh at the very idea that a robot would tell that kind of a joke. To be programmed to tell one-liners or puns on demand, that was nothing special. But Otto's limerick was disarmingly multifaceted.

This was something that Cade, who had not laughed, proceeded to explain in detail:

"A complex performance of humor," he said. "To fully appreciate it, one must first be familiar with the structure of a limerick, so that they might predict the vulgarity of the fourth line based on the final word of the third line. Only then will they find themselves susceptible to the most important element of comedy: surprise. When the final two lines of the limerick finish the story in an unexpected way, the listener laughs with shock at the difference between his lewd expectations and the mundane actuality."

There was bemused silence, until Drew said, "Yes, thank you, Cade, that was very insightful."

One of the engineers explained, "We brought Otto so that we could see how our robots interact with your androids. We've grown quite dependent on the robots, and it will take years, if not decades, to phase them all out and replace them with androids, so they'll need to get along in the meantime."

Cade approached Otto and said, "You and I are brothers, just as the Velb and the Vude are brothers, descended from a common ancestor."

"I'm pleased to meet you!" Otto said. "I'm sorry that I thought you were a human earlier, but you are visually indistinguishable from one. May I scan you?"

"I'm not sure that is allowed at this time," Cade said. "Many of my components are proprietary, and a contract has not yet been signed by–"

"It's alright," Drew said. "The important stuff is encrypted." He looked to the others in the room sheepishly, as if to say, *What a pain, always keeping everything on the up-and-up for the corporations, right?*

Otto scanned Cade. "Ooh, he has a contactless interface! That's very advanced!"

"Is it compatible with Otto's model?" an engineer asked.

To demonstrate, Cade placed his hand very near to Otto's chestplate, not quite touching, for a few seconds. Otto said, "I think it worked," but he said it in a language that the Minister did not understand.

"That's the Vude language," Anvar explained. Cade had changed

Otto's default language without needing a cable or a local wireless connection. An engineer remarked, "Useful."

"What about hazardous environments?" the other engineer asked, impatient to move along from what he saw as less essential social capacities. "We can send our robots into mineshafts, irradiated areas. How do your androids hold up?"

Finally, this meeting was going to a place where Drew could engage with relative confidence. He had responses to anticipated questions such as this one memorized, and spoke the Velb language with more confidence now. "Our androids are built inside and out to perform despite extreme heat, extreme cold, and radiation, plus anywhere you wouldn't send a human due to lack of oxygen: mines, underwater, high altitudes."

"And the quality of their performance does not deteriorate in those environments?"

"Not at all; we have tested them in all these conditions, both under remote control and with the proxy helmets – for when you want to be sure that specialized actions are being carried out according to the level of skill that a human expert possesses, in real time."

The Minister asked, "Can you show us the proxy helmet?"

"Absolutely." Drew picked up the bulky bag that Cade had carried in, and from it pulled a pair of gloves, which he slipped his hands into. Then he removed from the bag a thick cap bristling with wires, with a pair of black goggles attached.

"Now, this is my personal prototype of our latest model," Drew explained. "By the time you start receiving these, they will be consumer-grade, much prettier. The neural interface is painless and intuitive – very little training is needed to operate one of these."

Also in the bag were two more sets of much smaller goggles, which Cade handed to the Minister and to one of the engineers. Drew hauled the clunky helmet onto his head. Before lowering the goggles he looked to Cade, who nodded dutifully. Taking control of Cade's operations was not something Drew enjoyed doing – though he had no problem performing the operation with any other android

– but Cade, of course, did not object, taking both the action itself and the philosophical implications of it in stride.

"Cade, could you please stand with your hands at your sides, and do nothing else until I've connected to you."

Cade did so, while Drew tightened the straps on the helmet and the cuffs on the gloves, before engaging the somewhat involved sequence that activated the manual override. "I'm just going to have Cade do a few simple actions. You can watch my point of view through those goggles. With this amount of equipment, I can move Cade around this room easily enough, but there are additional pieces of equipment, treadmills and full-body suits and so on, which can facilitate a journey of any length and the precise movement of any limb." As it was, Drew demonstrated how, by lifting his hand, he could command Cade to lift his own hand. He had Cade move to the table full of tools, pick several of them up, and utilize them dexterously.

"What about feedback?" an engineer asked. "Is there any feedback?"

"The feedback is complete and accurate, even without the full-body suit. With just the helmet and its neural interface, I can not only see what Cade sees, but feel anything he feels. For example, if he were to step on a sharp rock, I would feel that as keenly as if I had stepped on it myself, because the helmet connects my brain to all of his sensory input."

Drew removed the helmet, and held it out to the Minister. "Would you like a demonstration?"

The Minister set aside the goggles and took the helmet gingerly, as though he were afraid he might break it. One of the scientists stepped forward to help him put it on.

Drew stood next to Cade. "Can you see what Cade sees?" he asked the Minister, once he'd got the helmet adjusted.

"Oh yes." The Minster looked all around, and with no perceptible delay, so did Cade, swiveling his head in every direction.

"Can you see me? Go ahead and have Cade take my pulse."

The Minister reached out, so that Cade would extend his hand to

Drew's throat. When the Minister curled his third and fourth fingers against his palm, Cade did the same, and when the Minister's hand nudged forward a final few inches, Cade's hand fell precisely on Drew's carotid artery.

"Ha! I do feel it," the Minister said, and then imitated the pulse's speed by saying, "*Thump-thump, thump-thump*, yes, that's uncanny."

"What about the extreme temperatures or hazardous materials that the android will be working in?" an engineer asked. "Would the human controller not also experience these sensations?"

"The feedback can be calibrated so that conditions which would harm a human, but not the android, register at lower levels. For example, if he is repairing a piece of equipment in a polar snowstorm, the goggles will display the actual temperature of anything he handles, but the feeling will only register to his controller as 'pretty cold.' This is so that anomalous changes to the temperature of an object, or the ambient temperature, can still be detected instantly, and dealt with."

The engineers had many more questions, and the Minister had a few as well, and Drew answered them – and demonstrated with Cade – as far as he was able, without giving away any industry secrets. One day the Velb would reverse-engineer an android of their own, but Drew was obligated to keep all the secrets he could, to extend the demand for Vude's products as far as possible.

When the engineers and Minister were satisfied, they consulted briefly with Anvar. "My aide has just a few more questions," the Minister said, "and provided the answers are satisfactory, we are happy to arrange a purchase. Vude should transmit the contracts to my ministry with all speed." With that, he and the engineers excused themselves, and Anvar invited Drew and Cade to have a seat at a table. He sat across them, pen in hand and ready to take notes.

"I'll be frank with you," Anvar said, "I'm here to talk about the aspects of this negotiation that are, shall we say, beneath the Minister's dignity."

After a moment of thought, translating Anvar's words in his head, Drew realized what Anvar was probably talking about. But he didn't want to just come right out and say it, in case he was mistaken. Slowly, he responded, "You want to know if our androids are..."

"Are they fully functional, yes," Anvar said, with the smirk of someone who was only asking these questions because he was ranked too low in the organization to weasel out of it.

Drew nodded matter-of-factly. "Save for the features I described to the Minster, all of our androids are indistinguishable from humans, and that includes genitalia."

Cade said nothing as he sat there next to Drew; he appeared attentive but offered no responses, as he was not being addressed directly. Again, Drew regretted that Cade was being talked about like he was a product – even if that was admittedly what he was.

"And how does one calibrate the strength they exert?" Anvar asked.

"By default, all androids have the strength of an adult human in prime physical condition. In emergency situations, they will exert greater strength, say, to lift a heavy object off of a human who is trapped beneath it. But in normal circumstances, it requires deliberate calibration on the part of the owner to adjust strength, and even then, that is only industrial licensees, and some commercial. We don't give consumer-level androids the ability to terrorize the community at the whim of a vengeful owner...if that's what you're asking."

Anvar gave an ambiguous roll of his shoulders, then explained, "We've just had some problems with our robots, ah, hurting some consumers."

"In what way? If you have specific concerns, I can address them one by one."

"After the initial release, we had consumers making unauthorized anatomical modifications to the robots."

Only then did it occur to Drew that they were still talking about sex. "Giving them...private parts, you mean."

"Indeed. And that resulted in some terrible accidents. Electrocution, perforation. I won't go into detail, suffice it to say it got gruesome. And yet despite that, I'm sure I hardly need to point out to you the human propensity to have sex with everything imaginable."

At last, Drew allowed himself a little good-natured laugh, only to make it clear to Anvar that he was sympathetic. "It's the same way on Vude, yes."

Anvar went on: "So our manufacturers started making rudimentary genitalia standard on all consumer-level robot models. Pressurized tubes for both models; it's just a matter of which direction the tube is pressurized from, you know what I mean? Anyway, the reasoning was, if they could regulate the robot genitalia, they could maintain strict safety standards, and eliminate the need for underground manufacturing. And it's mostly worked, but the fact is, even if they talk and act like humans, robots are still machines, which means they can still be hacked, and they can still malfunction. Every once in a while, some poor horny bastard's pelvis gets crushed. Which is why it is extremely important that your androids are capable of sexual intercourse with humans, and just as important that a human can *safely* have sex with one. If the human cares to. And they probably do."

"Every android comes standard with biometric feedback scanners to keep themselves attuned to any humans they have contact with. They are also kinematically redundant. Thus, regardless of whether a human begins to shout 'faster, faster, harder, harder,' an android will not obey with hazardous force or velocity. You can give the Minister my personal reassurance that our androids are safe to have sex with."

Anvar raised an eyebrow. "Your *personal* reassurance?"

Drew reflexively looked over at Cade, then quickly corrected himself, and faced forward. "I would appreciate it if you do not take this as a testimonial meant for public consumption," Drew said. "But yes."

For all their formalities, the Velb were hospitable people, and offered Drew and Cade a night's rest in the luxurious guests' quarters at the

Ministry before they made the journey back to Vude. They even offered Cade his own room. Cade was indifferent to this, but accepted graciously for show. For his part, Drew was thrilled to sleep in a soft bed for a night, instead of a spartan bunk on a transport ship.

Anvar called for a junior staff member to show the two of them to their rooms. On the way there, Drew couldn't keep himself from mulling over all the ways he had embarrassed himself during the demonstration, pronouncing Velb words incorrectly and at one point simply tripping over his own two feet. To fight these thoughts off, he tried to focus on the thing he'd enjoyed most: Otto.

It had been a long time since Drew had interacted with a robot. He, of course, had spent the last ten years perfecting androids like Cade in order to make robots obsolete, but that didn't mean he didn't *like* robots. He'd always adored them: their imperfect imitations of human voices, their stilted movements, their clunky charm. Androids were a monumental achievement, but they were so perfectly human that they could get kind of boring.

"I really liked that Otto," Drew remarked to Cade.

"I noticed this," Cade deadpanned.

"Did *you* like him?"

"I can understand why humans find him charming," Cade said. "His exaggerated physical gestures and vocal mannerisms are designed to be appealing to humans. This is because the Velb have not yet been able to achieve your level of realism in their humanoid constructs. Rather than build robots whose appearance and movements would lie in the 'uncanny valley,' and repulse humans, the Velb scaled back to a lower level of realism, making their robots 'loveable' instead."

Drew knew that Cade did not need to be as clinical, as analytical, as he was being. It was a tone he adopted when he knew that his actual, blunt opinion would hurt a human's feelings. "I know you're not jealous of Otto," he teased Cade. "Otto might get more smiles and laughs, but you're the true marvel. You're so marvelous, people don't even realize you're marvelous."

"I'm aware of this," Cade said, suspiciously free of inflection.

"Everything that Otto does was programmed into him, including that joke. What I do, what I say, is informed by my experiences, and thus more nuanced. I am a thinking, learning being, but he is simply a machine. I am superior to him."

You didn't have to agree with me quite that hard, Drew thought, and felt a bit silly now for liking Otto at all. But all of that was true: even if Cade could not truly experience emotions, he could learn what they meant and how to express them with more nuance – and that included defensiveness. Drew could do nothing but chuckle at Cade's jealous assertion.

Drew ordered the most expensive food on the room service menu, billed it to his superiors back on Vude, and savored every tasty bite as he mused on the events of the day – but mostly Otto. Even after he'd made himself sleepy eating too much dinner, Drew found himself smiling into his pillow as he lay in bed, thinking about how fun Otto had been, his funny joke, his voice with its endearingly mechanical inflections.

And he thought about what Anvar had said, about all the Velb robots, presumably including Otto, being anatomically correct.

Drew knew he was being silly, thinking about this; Cade had a perfectly agreeable penis, thick and shapely and practiced at satisfying him without fail. As an android, Cade possessed strength and stamina beyond human capability; he could lift and bounce Drew however he liked, and always in a safe, carefully regulated way. Why, when he had Cade, would Drew want to have sex with a metal robot with a rudimentary penis and an apparent tendency to injure those he penetrated?

Drew felt a little shudder of a thrill, thinking of it. That was precisely it, wasn't it? It would be strange, inhuman, and a little risky, and that's exactly why it piqued his curiosity.

Of course, those Velb who'd suffered misfortune in their determination to have exotic sex with robots had made stupid mistakes. But

Drew had an expert understanding of humanoid constructs, how they functioned and how to interact with them. If *he* tried, he could enjoy all the power and strength of a robot without putting himself in danger. He was certain *he* would be able to slide that robot cock inside him and feel that unyielding metal against his skin and still walk away unharmed.

And surely Cade wouldn't mind. Although Drew had not been with anyone else since he had built Cade, Cade couldn't actually feel jealousy, so there was no reason not to seek out a robot, just this one time.

Drew was not sure how he might track down Otto at this point, but he figured he could just ask around a little, make up some phony excuse. And if not Otto, any robot would probably do. So he got up, dressed, and wandered down the corridor until he came to a junction, where a concierge was sitting at a desk.

"I beg your pardon, sorry," he said, haltingly, in Velb. "I'm the scientist from Vude. I did a demonstration for the Minister of Commerce today."

"Yes, of course, what can I do for you?"

"During the demonstration, a robot was brought in, a robot named Otto. I've just thought of something I'd like to see Otto for. Could you contact someone from the lab for me, to see about that?"

"No need," said the concierge. "Your android asked to see Otto just a little while ago. I had him sent over. I thought the android was making the request on your behalf. I hope that wasn't a mistake?"

Drew did not want to hint that anything might be amiss, so he hid his surprise and said, "Not at all. I forgot that I'd asked him to do that. I'll just head back to Cade's room, then, thank you."

He hurried back down the corridor, not sure if he should be panicking. For what possible reason could Cade have asked to see Otto? Drew was as susceptible as anyone else to ascribing human emotions to androids, even though he knew better than anyone that it was impossible. Cade would certainly not lure Otto into his room to dismantle him in a jealous rage after seeing how much Drew liked him...

Would he?

Drew turned the handle on the Cade's door and pushed it open without knocking. As the door swung silently open, he was completely floored by the sight before him: Otto was flat on his back on the bed, his spindly metal legs spread across the enormous mattress. Cade was straddling Otto, facing away from him, his eyes on the door as it opened. He rode Otto hard; Otto's large but finely-articulated hands gripped Cade's hips tightly, slamming him down while his pelvis pounded upward, fucking Cade with enormous, perfectly rhythmic, force. It looked like far more than a human could take.

Drew was aghast. Of all the things he'd expected to see when he walked in, Cade riding Otto with abandon had not been on the list. But before he could utter a sound, Cade looked right at him and put a finger to his lips. Then he made a gesture with both hands, cupping them across the top of his head. It took Drew a moment to decipher this gesture: the proxy helmet!

Drew silently dipped out of the room and dashed next door. While he dug the helmet out of the bag, he was laughing with the joyous realization that Cade had not only recognized Drew's desire, but that he'd quite independently taken the initiative to resolve the situation in a way that would be both satisfactory and safe for him. Drew laid down on the bed and crammed the helmet onto his head.

The instant he secured the device, he was overcome with the sensation of being smoothly and powerfully fucked. Otto was driving into him up to the hilt, and he was able to take it beautifully, without pain. It was so intensely exciting, surrendering to a magnificently brutal assault from a robot; Drew indulged fearlessly in the feeling of being pierced by an unyielding cock, pounding deeply with blind vigor.

Drew briefly considered taking over control of Cade, but decided that he would rather sit back and let Cade continue to make the decisions – it might lend more of an element of surprise to what was happening. Not to mention, Drew was already drowning in such intense pleasure, it was unlikely that he could think clearly enough to switch the helmet over.

Through the goggles, Drew saw Cade's point of view shift slightly, and surmised that he had just changed positions, leaning forward and getting on his hands and knees so Otto could take him from behind. Otto's grip loosened for a moment, until Cade had fully assumed the position, at which point Otto clutched him even harder around his hips and continued slamming into him. Drew was absolutely sure that if he were to take a pounding this hard from someone with a rigid metal body, his entire spine would be pulverized to dust; but experiencing it through Cade, all he felt was the exhilarating sensation of a relentless and well-lubed cock deep inside him, deliciously pummeling his prostate.

The friction was just right, and the occasional clank of metal on metal staggeringly provocative. Drew wallowed in how joyfully nasty it was, to be bent over and taking it like this from a robot. At the same time, though, he was begging, silently, for Cade to know enough to turn over. Even if Cade was not sufficiently familiar with the minutiae of Drew's thought processes – and he was – surely he must be able to at least guess that Drew would want to have the most thorough, comprehensive experience possible, while he had the chance.

Cade did not let him down. When his view through the goggles spun, so that he was now looking at a white ceiling, Drew began to chant *yes, yes*, because a moment later, Otto came into view, looming over him as the intense fucking resumed. This was what Drew really wanted: to be able to *see* that it was a machine fucking him, to be able to grab at Otto's body, put his fingerprints on Otto's burnished surfaces while he got absolutely railed.

Cade was tilting his head slowly forward and back, giving Drew a good long look at Otto on top of him and between his thighs. Drew was so immersed in the visuals and the sensations, he himself was thrusting, rolling his hips, seeking the depth and speed he craved. And while every moment was electrified ecstasy, those moments when Cade did exactly what Drew did, felt exactly what Drew wanted to feel, were the most powerfully sublime. Drew moaned unabashedly, wondering if perhaps Cade could hear him in the next room.

Otto, tireless and cheerfully obedient, continued to pound away at Cade, who took it expertly. Drew was reduced to grunts as he felt the force of every thrust. The shock of cold metal against his skin dissipated as Otto was warmed by the heat that Cade's body produced. Drew clutched at the sheets. Even though it was already too much, had been too much from the first moment, it just kept building and building. A final burst of delicious sensation radiated from head to foot as Drew climaxed untouched, needing only the neural interface's input to drive him to a peak of ecstasy formerly reserved only for the deepest prostate orgasms.

About the time his sharp cries tapered off, Drew saw Cade put a hand on Otto's chest-plate, a command to halt. Drew was sure now that Cade had heard him getting very loud and then very quiet, and was grateful for that; he was uncertain whether he would have survived if the fucking had continued much longer after he'd climaxed.

Drew pulled the helmet off as Otto was withdrawing, and suddenly he was no longer a wild, heaving thing with his hands full of metal and his rim straining to accommodate a huge and relentless robot cock – though he was still an exhausted, sweaty mess for certain. He tugged off his damp pajama bottoms and made for the bathroom, to take a long shower. There, he worked out his confusion, feeling worn-out and satisfied even though he was not – as was usually the case after that much intensity – nursing weakened quadriceps, a tender hole, and a sore prostate.

When Drew returned from the bathroom, he got one more surprise: Cade was sitting up in his bed, perusing the guest suite's little complimentary guide to local sights and events. He was neatly dressed and groomed, his appearance in no way hinting at what he'd been doing. Drew could not even bring himself to comment on what Cade had done for him, not to tease nor to express gratitude; he was still so overwhelmed, and a little embarrassed as well, by how filthy it had been. Instead he gestured in the vague direction of next door and asked, "You didn't care to have a nice room all to yourself?"

"I was lonely without you," was all Cade said in reply.

THE JOB THAT TOOK HIM BEYOND THE STARS

Angelo was terrified that he might not be allowed to eat in Chicago for ten years.

Perhaps it would be more accurate to say that he would not be allowed to eat in any *meaningful* way in Chicago for ten years. But Chicago was his home, and if the slightest suspicion arose today that he was an Earlen inspector, he would not be able to review a restaurant in Chicago for a decade, which would mean even more time on the road. He'd just been recruited by Earlen two months ago, and already his new career, his dream job, was in jeopardy.

He wouldn't have been so worried, but the giveaways to his identity just seemed to be cascading today. First, his dining partner, Justin, had gone out of town on short notice, on account of a family member who had passed away. Perfectly understandable, but it left Angelo here, a well-dressed man dining alone, ordering the same meal he had ordered the last time he'd been here. He wished he had a briefcase, some papers, a laptop, to at least make it seem like he was dining alone because he was traveling on business. But tonight it would be just him and the food.

The result was that Angelo could not imagine a more obvious Earlen inspector than him at this moment, and his nervousness about the matter was certainly making things worse. Who would be sweating about eating at the same restaurant twice and dining alone, unless they had something to hide?

And all of this was before he saw a waiter staring at him and fidgeting.

It wasn't his waiter. It was another one, who had caught sight of him and then seemed to become fixated. When the waiter stepped away for a moment, Angelo was sure that he was telling the chef that an Earlen inspector was here. Chefs and restaurant owners often complained about the anxiety they suffered over their status with Earlen, and how that status might change from year to year. Angelo hated being a part of that effect.

All through his meal, Angelo could barely concentrate, distracted as he was by the mysterious waiter, who soon came back into view and then seemed to loom closer with each passing minute. The last few bites of his meal he just shoveled into his mouth, wanting desperately for this dinner to be over, to leave and to hope that no one at Earlen found out that his cover had been blown. But when the bill was brought to him, it was not his waiter, it was the one who had been staring at him.

Angelo grabbed his coat, handed the waiter two hundred dollars in cash, and started to say "I don't need any change," but then the waiter sat across from him at the table.

"I think you might be able to help me," the waiter said. Angelo noticed that he had a few beads of sweat along his hairline.

"I'm afraid you're mistaken," Angelo replied. "I'm in no position to do any favors for anyone, and anything you think about me that gave you that impression, I hope you will put those suspicions out of your mind."

The waiter laced and unlaced his fingers, and blinked at Angelo's panic. "You're new here, huh? That's fine, but we don't have much time."

Angelo was taken aback. How had the waiter known that? How many nervous rookie Earlen inspectors had he seen? Angelo did not even know what to say. "I don't...have to respond to that," he stammered.

"I understand, I understand." The waiter moved one hand to cover his heart, then tucked in his thumb and little finger, with his other three fingers pointing to his left. What did that mean? Was than an "E," for Earlen?

Or was it a symbol for some sort of organization? Was this waiter a spy? Was he in organized crime? Was the mob now leaning on Earlen inspectors to give their front restaurants good reviews? That had not been mentioned during Angelo's orientation.

The waiter must have taken Angelo's wide-eyed stare for recognition, because he then said, "I need you to come with me right now. I have urgent business. *Urgent business*. You understand?"

Angelo understood that if he didn't do what this man said, he would probably be killed, or worse, so he nodded, and followed the waiter as he got up and headed for the exit that led to the hotel. "I have a room here," the waiter said, which seemed odd, but then again, he wasn't a waiter, was he, he was a goon, or a made man, or something like that. The terminology had probably changed since those gangster movies had come out when he was a kid.

As they got on the elevator, staring straight ahead and standing perfectly still, Angelo had a glimmer of hope: perhaps he had misinterpreted the situation, and the waiter wasn't with the mob; maybe he was a spy after all. If that were the case, Angelo thought, he was at least about to die in a much cooler way.

The waiter brought him into a room in the hotel which appeared untouched: no suitcase, an undisturbed bed. Immediately, the waiter began stripping off his clothes. "I'm sorry to do this to you, but I'm in heat and I need your help with it. It wasn't supposed to happen, I thought I was years away in my cycle." Angelo watched, frozen in terror, as the waiter first got completely naked, and then grabbed at his midsection and pulled his skin away in three vigorous motions – his human skin. Beneath it was a mottled hide of shifting colors. "I'm Lu'uk, by the way. Well, what are you waiting for? Get your skin off and help me! I'm in agony."

Angelo could do nothing but hold out his arms and shake his head, to indicate his utter uselessness.

Lu'uk's gold eyes got wide. "Oh, no. You mean you're not a Zohrr?"

"I don't even know what that is."

The frills around Lu'uk's jaw drooped. "But the way you were acting in the restaurant. Like you were uncomfortable in your skin. And then being all coy about what was going on with you..."

"That's just who I am as a person," Angelo said, "I'm sorry."

"Shit. Shit, shit. Well, I hope you can keep a secret, then. Sorry to spring one of this level on you. Listen, you're not the ideal candidate I thought you were, but you can probably still help me, at least for long enough for me to find a Zohrr who has a suppressant on them. You'll help a guy out, right? It's not going to cost you any money, and no one will ever know." Lu'uk ducked into the bathroom, where Trevor could see him grabbing an armful of towels.

"I feel like I don't have a choice," Angelo called after him.

"You do," Lu'uk said as he darted back into the room and spread the towels on the bed, "but let's pretend you don't, okay? That will simplify things."

Angelo's heart had been pumping nothing but adrenaline and he had not had a single coherent thought for at least half an hour. Andt that wasn't all very weird, but frankly nothing that Lu'uk could say or do at this point could panic him any more than he had been the moment he'd thought that his cover as an Earlen inspector was blown. All Angelo wanted to do was go home and write his review like nothing out of the ordinary had happened, and cooperating with this being from another world seemed to be his ticket to doing that, so he clasped his hands together to indicate his willingness and said, "Okay, what do I do?"

"Alright, so Zohrr go into heat once every," Lu'uk waved his hand, "something-something years. I don't remember what it is in Earth years. That's probably why I'm in this mess. When this happens we have to mate, like we *have* to. If you were another Zohrr, right now we'd be having a super intense physical altercation to determine which one of us is going to drop some eggs and which one is going to fertilize them. But since you don't have any eggs, that's already kind of been decided. So the first thing you need to do is help me get the eggs out."

Lu'uk grabbed Angelo's hand and pulled him onto the bed. With a little guidance from Lu'uk, they laid down on their sides, facing each other. Angelo was still fully-clothed, and Lu'uk was not doing anything to change that; Angelo kept his mouth shut and followed along. His eyes followed Lu'uk's hands as he reached down and showed Angelo a slit at the apex of his thighs. He tugged it open a little with his fingertips. "Put your fingers in here. You have to massage it to make the eggs come out."

"You want me to just...put my fingers..."

"Please," Lu'uk whined, "it's not gonna bite."

The urgency in Lu'uk's voice shook the fear from Angelo. This was a being who was clearly in genuine distress, and it was within his power to help. Angelo reached out and dipped his fingers into the slit.

"Oh, yes, yes, *oh*."

Lu'uk was smooth and delicate inside. At first, Angelo's exploring fingers felt only the muscles of Lu'uk's slick inner walls as they fluttered and contracted. But as he went deeper, his fingertips caressed something round and firm. "I think I feel it," he said.

"Good. Just keep rubbing, and it'll come down and you can take it out."

Sure enough, Angelo found that as he massaged Lu'uk inside, he had to keep sliding further out to accommodate the egg's journey. Then, he could slip his fingers around it, and pull it out into the open air. It was transparent, about the size of a golf ball, with some ghostly gold matter in the center.

"What do I do with it?"

"Just set it on the towel, it's fine."

Angelo did as he was told. "Is that all?"

"There's a few more," Lu'uk said with a grimace. "Just keep doing what you're doing."

As Angelo put his fingers back in, it became apparent to him that for Lu'uk, this was more than just relief, it was pleasure. But perhaps he was projecting; Lu'uk was making exciting noises in reaction to

Angelo's prodding and exploring, and he was so warm and slippery inside, Angelo couldn't help but get a little turned on, himself. He found the whole thing very compelling. As he worked for the second egg, his fear vanished, and he focused on his task; he found it not repulsive at all, but primal and erotic. He pressed deep, and when he brushed a spot with his fingers that made Lu'uk shudder, he reflexively wanted to do it again, immediately. Lu'uk was gooey and warm inside, and his instructions sounded sexual: "Deeper." "Grab it." "Do it for me, please."

It became increasingly apparent that this experience was indeed meant to be pleasurable. With each successive egg that he removed, Lu'uk squirmed harder and moaned louder. Finally, when the fifth egg slid out with the help of Angelo's slippery fingers, Lu'uk was overcome by a climactic shudder. An additional gush of fluid accompanied this last egg that Angelo extracted. The mess dripped all over Angelo's hand and wrist, and this release provoked a gasp of gratification from Lu'uk.

"Okay," Lu'uk sighed, "that's it, I think."

Angelo looked at the little clutch of glistening eggs on the towel. "Now what?"

"Now you need to fertilize them."

"I need to what?"

"Relax. Nothing's going to happen. There's no incubation chamber around here. It's just, I'm kind of empathically linked with these eggs, and so I won't be able to calm down until I know that someone else has put their genetic material on them. So if you'll allow me..."

Lu'uk unbuckled Angelo's belt, unzipped his trousers, and took out his cock, which was rigid and throbbing. For a moment, Angelo was embarrassed that Lu'uk now knew that he'd found the egg extraction process arousing – perhaps a Zohrr would think that was disrespectful? But then, he supposed that his state of arousal was pretty integral to what Lu'uk apparently wanted him to do.

Lu'uk gave Angelo a nudge to pivot him so that he was aiming properly, then began to stroke him off. It was unceremonious, and his palm was a little rough, but Angelo didn't need anything fancy; Lu'uk worked him expertly and tirelessly, until Angelo's whole body shook and he shot three long streaks of ejaculate onto the eggs.

As soon as this was done, Lu'uk rolled onto his back and slumped on the mattress. "Thank you. Thank you so much. I feel so much better." But only relaxed for a moment before taking a deep breath and sat up a little, propping himself on his elbows. "For now, anyway. I've never tried it half-way like this, with a non-Zohrr partner. Hopefully it'll all be good, and I won't have to worry again for a while."

Angelo looked at Lu'uk, then looked at the eggs, then at Lu'uk's glistening slit, then at the eggs again. "Forgive me for asking, but did we just have sex? Did I just have sex with an alien?"

"We did a little bit, yeah." Lu'uk got up from the bed, then bent down over the eggs to wrap them up in the towel.

"So, you're an alien from another planet, and you just...work in a restaurant?"

Lu'uk scoffed as he carried the bundle into the bathroom. He called over his shoulder, "You actually think that the aliens that visit Earth are infiltrating the royal families of Europe and becoming presidents and prime ministers, carrying out some evil agenda in the halls of power? You watch too much television." He came back into the room, picked up his discarded skin off the floor, and leaned on the desk as he tried to smooth it out a little. "I'm just bumming around here for a while before it's time for me to go back to school and pick a career. By the way, you can take off whenever you want to. It takes me like a half hour to put my human suit on, so I'll be here a while."

Angelo kind of wanted to stay; he had a million more questions for Lu'uk. But he was, to begin with, not one hundred percent sure that this was not a weird dream or hallucination, or a very, very elaborate scam. And even if it was real, he was also not sure if he was welcome to stay if he cared to. He put himself away, buttoned up his trousers, and buckled his belt before he rolled off the bed. As he walked toward the door, Lu'uk held out his hand for Angelo to shake. "Thanks again, I really do appreciate what you did."

Angelo shook his hand, and said, "Can I give you some advice? On that whole picking-a-career thing?"

"Sure."

"Get out of the restaurant business before you get so good at it that they want you to be an Earlen inspector." Angelo looked away and sighed. "It's really been a minefield for me so far."

AND THEN THERE WAS THE ONE ABOUT...

THE CHATTY SHUTTLEMATES

RHEM'S HOPES of a quiet shuttle ride were dashed when he found out that the two passengers he would be sharing a compartment with were Prodians. Prodians couldn't stand a moment's silence; every time Rhem had encountered one, they would talk his ear off, prattling on about any little thing just to have some talking. To be fair, they could also be excellent listeners, if *you* had something to say. They just needed to have constant chatter.

So instead of getting some well-deserved (if you were to ask him) sleep, Rhem resigned himself to looking out the window, watching his homeworld grow slowly closer as the shuttle blasted off from the orbital station. He had a hard time falling asleep when anything more raucous than an ambient hum was present. He covered himself with his jacket, like a makeshift blanket, even though he knew it was no use.

As Rhem collapsed into his seat, the Prodians paused in their conversation to greet him cheerily, but as soon as it became apparent to them that he was not in the mood to converse, they went back to gabbing with each other. "I was looking at the brochures on the way here," one of them said, "and I'm not sure I'm going to be able to stay a whole Earth-year. Things are more expensive than I thought they were. I'm going to run out of money before a year is up, for sure."

The other Prodian reassured him, "If you have the money to get to Earth, you'll be able to stay there as long as you want. I spent two years on Earth when I was as young as you, even though I showed up with practically nothing."

"But I don't want to get a job!"

Rhem rolled his eyes when he heard this, and tried, but failed, to tune them out.

"Oh, you don't have to get a job, silly!" A Prodian laugh was always irritatingly high and staccato. "You use what you've got. Here's what you do: first you find a man. That's a male human."

Rhem was suddenly terrified that he would be brought into the conversation, but neither of the Prodians acknowledged him at all. He slowly relaxed again as the lesson stayed between them. It continued, with the elder instructing the younger:

"Now, you know your tentacle?"

Another giggle, this one more demure. "Yes...."

"Men have a tentacle too, but they don't have much control over theirs at all. It's ridiculous; they act like it doesn't even belong to them, but it's quite firmly attached. Anyway, what I found is, if you wrap your tentacle around a man's tentacle, and squeeze it just right, they really like that."

"How do you know that?"

"A man asked me to do it once...and then he asked me to do it a lot more!"

"Stop, you're so weird! Okay, so what happens next?"

"Oh, there's all sorts of things that men like. You can unroll your tongue all the way, and men have lots of places you can put it. And you can ask the man to put his tentacle just about anywhere, too. I'm serious, you can just, like, bend your arm, and have him put his tentacle in the crook of it, and they think that is the wildest thing, just because they're not used to being around Prodians."

"But how is all this supposed to get me enough money to stay on Earth?"

Rhem burst out laughing at the naiveté of the younger one. When they stopped to stare at him, he pretended he was only coughing, and excused himself. He wanted to sleep so badly, but instead he had to listen to all this. The older Prodian then went on to answer the question:

"Alright, so after you play with his tentacle a couple times, or let him play with yours, you tell him that you're so sad because you don't have any money to stay on Earth. You can't afford a place to live, you can't afford to eat a nice meal. You really don't want to leave, because the man has been so nice to you, and so *generous*. And the man won't want you to leave, because he likes playing with you so much. So if he can, he'll give you money, maybe twelve thousand credits, enough for you to get an apartment and buy some food. And that's on top of taking you out to restaurants and buying you fancy gifts."

"Twelve thousand credits! You could live for a month off of that on Earth, easily, couldn't you?" (Rhem concealed his disdain, staring out the window as he began to seethe. He would love to have twelve thousand credits a month to live on, let alone to give away to a bit on the side.) "But what if I find a man and he likes me, but he doesn't have twelve thousand credits to give me?"

"It's not that much of a problem. You can just find *two* men, and if they each give you six thousand credits, you'll be perfectly well off. You'll have to be careful, though, because men can get jealous, so you have to keep them a secret from each other, and keep track of what you did to each one, and not accidentally talk about what you did to one in front of the other. It's a little more work, but men are really fun, so if you have two to have fun with, so much the better. Sometimes one will like you to do stuff with *his* tentacle, and the other would rather you do things to him with *your* tentacle. They like how our tentacles can stretch out long, or get shorter and thick. And they all very much like it when you extend your tongue all the way and do things to them. It can be a lot of work, but they make the best noises when you do it, and their bodies are so fuzzy and nice."

Glad to know you're getting something out of it too, Rhem mused, *you know, besides twelve thousand credits a month.*

"Oh, well that doesn't sound so bad, then, to have two. But if I can't find two men who each have six thousand credits to spare? I feel like that's still a lot of money, just to give as a gift."

"Hmm, well I suppose then you'd have to find *four* men, and after you please them, ask them each for *three* thousand credits."

Rhem slumped down in his seat, pulled his jacket up over his head, and closed his eyes. "Hey, guys," he said, "I'm gonna try to take a nap now, but do me a favor and wake me up if you get down to a hundred credits a pop before the shuttle docks, okay?"

NO MATTER HOW MANY GENERATIONS

I HAD NEVER CARED to hear my family or my teachers talk about what life was like back on Earth, any more than my seven-times-great grandparents would have cared to hear my nine-times-great grandparents go on and on about crossing the American plains in a covered wagon. I was like any youth, convinced that the only interesting time and place was the one I was currently inhabiting, and loath to listen to any past generation's prattling about their privations or achievements.

I felt particularly justified in my self-centered attitudes and disinterest in others' lives once I entered medical school. Not only was I smug about my path to one of society's most high-status careers, but every waking moment was now taken up with studying, lectures, and training at the robotic surgery machines. I simply did not have time to care about anything or anyone else. And when I had a few weeks' break one summer, and took a shuttle back to my parents' house, I did not want to do anything but sleep in and laze around. I definitely did not want to waste my precious relaxation time with my great-uncle Jules.

"He's got something very important to talk to you about," my mother said, standing in the doorway to my room. "He's come all the way from Yendar One to see you."

I didn't like to make my mother unhappy, so I hauled myself out of bed and shuffled into the dining room, where Uncle Jules was sitting at the table with several battered storage containers piled up next to him.

"Look at you, all grown up!" he said when I appeared. "Last time I saw you, you were yay-big." He gestured to indicate that I had indeed been much shorter at age six. "Have a seat."

Instead of doing this, I got some coffee, but he kept talking to me while I poured: "I owe you an apology. I put this visit off for too long. To be honest, I had hoped, and almost had reason to believe, that I might not have to do this at all." When I came back to the table with the coffee, he thanked me and reached out for it. I sighed, handed it over, and poured myself another. He went on. "And I didn't come here to interrupt your studies, to throw your life into disarray..."

This reassurance was sufficiently incongruous to finally grab my attention. I sat down and listened more carefully.

"...Rather, I'm here to prepare you for what *is* going to do those things."

"Well, whatever it is, it's picked a terrible time. I've only got one year left of school, and then I'll be trying to start a practice."

"That's part of the problem," he said. "It was only when I heard that you were studying to be a doctor that I knew I needed to see you. Prior to that, I had been in denial, convinced that our family had escaped its fate when we left Earth."

"I hope you didn't come all the way here to tell me dumb Earth stories," I said. "Although I might appreciate the help getting back to sleep; I've got a lot of it to catch up on."

The way Uncle Jules was glaring at me, however, told me that it was not as boring as all that, and perhaps I had better stop being a smart-mouth for a few minutes. "If you'll allow me to explain," he said. "Hopefully the story of what will soon be *your* life will be enough to keep you interested."

He took one of the storage units from his stack and unsealed it. It opened with a hiss, and inside were ancient and yellowed but very tidy bundles, wrapped with ribbon.

"These are books," Uncle Jules explained. "Or rather, these are what books used to be." He lifted one out of its custom-sized compartment and untied the ribbon, then invited me to open it. "Written by one of our ancestors, hundreds of years ago."

I flipped open the cover, to find that the first page – and the hundreds of successive pages – were filled margin-to-margin with handwriting.

"Not many people can read handwriting from this period anymore," Uncle Jules said. "Thankfully, they were transcribed long ago, and you can read everything that's written here on a crystal display." He handed me a thin, compact Reader, not as nice as the one I already had. I flicked it on, and began to read the words aloud. "Contained herein is the most complete record of my years with the great–"

"SH!" Uncle Jules silenced me harshly. "Don't say the name out loud." He took the Reader from me and set it on the table. "We don't know for a fact that saying his name is one of the ways to summon him, but we don't like to take any chances."

"Summoning? What?"

Uncle Jules sighed, rested his elbows on the table, folded his hands, and closed his eyes. "This is all very confusing, I know. I will begin at the beginning. When your ancestor was not much older than you are now, he met a very unusual man, seemingly by chance, and almost immediately thereafter, declared an undying devotion to him. The man was, I suppose you could call him an oracle: he could take one look at a person and know everything about them. He had a window into the dark heart of humanity, and his fascination with us became his life's work. In these memoirs, our ancestor describes the relationship as a companionate one, but the way he explains it – the abject adoration, the utter devotion – he seems to not understand his own situation. His entire life revolved around this man, and he seemed to only shake free of this servitude very late in his life.

"These memoirs detail the man's extraordinary powers, and describe many strange adventures. Some of the feats he was renowned for may not seem so impressive to us now, but he did them without using machines or cyber-enhancement. Imagine having been *born* with infrared and thermal vision, being able to look into people's minds and souls, seeing the trails they leave as they move through the world. That was this man's ability. And his exploits might have survived only as a collection of tall tales about an eccentric genius, but as one century rolled into another, the very same man appeared again, and entangled himself with the memoirist's direct descendant. He performed the same feats, demonstrated the same superhuman abilities, and won the same worship from his chosen acolyte.

"A generation later, it happened again. And then again, and soon a hundred years had gone by, and still our family played host to a man with an unchanging appearance and a mind beyond the understanding of ordinary people, an ethereal being who inhabited a liminal half-world where everything was linear, logical, and clear. I don't know when exactly we truly understood that we were dealing with a creature not of our Earth. Every one of our antecedents who chronicled their lives with this being continued to refer to it only as a person in their writings. But no matter how many generations this being inhabited a human form, he never accepted human limitations, and repeatedly expressed astonishment that humans could not do everything he did. At some point, once our family finally came to understand that this was our fate, it became a tradition to train up successive descendants, to methodically prepare them for a life of devotion whenever the being returned."

Uncle Jules placed his hand on the Reader as he finally opened his eyes again. "You can feel that, I think, when you read the stories of the later generations. A voice in the writing speaks of an eternal inevitability, an unbroken chain through the centuries, which gives each story, even the earliest ones, a strange timelessness."

Uncle Jules took another storage unit from the stack, a much smaller one this time. Unsealing it, he removed an uneven bundle of mismatched pictures.

"We only have a few images of what we are certain is the being. He did not care to be photographed. There are numerous artists' renderings." He handed me the photos. "You can see its Earthly guise remains much the same over time, always more or less human."

The man in the pictures Jules showed me was invariably tall, thin to the point of being gaunt, and while dressed impeccably, gave off an aura of otherworldliness. If he was in a crowd, you wouldn't look at him twice, but if someone told you to pick out the one person in that crowd who was a supernatural entity in disguise, you'd definitely pick him.

"Is there a reason to be afraid of it?" I asked, as I examined the pictures.

"Most of us in the line have embraced our fate," Uncle Jules said. "Only a few of us decided to flee from it at all costs."

I put the pictures down. "That's why you came to Yendar One all those years ago, with Grandpa and Grandma and Mom?"

He nodded. "I didn't want to be a part of the tradition. When my grandfather told us about this thing, how it would slither into our lives and convince us to serve it, I refused to subject myself or the family line to such a fate any longer. We set out for the farthest colony, hoping against hope that whatever this *thing* was, it would not be able to find us. And as the years went by, we became increasingly certain that we were correct, that the being could not have followed us here through the vacuum of space, and we were free. But, I don't know, it may have stowed away on the ship. There's no way to tell."

"This thing is *here*?"

Uncle Jules lifted his hands. "I don't know that. I don't think anybody *can* know, until it manifests as a man. But your mother sent me a message, updating me on how the family was doing here on Yendar Three, and in it she mentioned you were studying medicine."

"Does that have something to do with it?"

"The one chosen is always in the medical profession. We don't know why. Perhaps it needs someone with a healer's point of view, or steady hands and a doctor's eye for detail. Perhaps he needs to have his medical needs taken care of by a trusted confidante, lest his true form be revealed to the world. But your pursuit of that career path tells me that the destiny of our family line may still be hopelessly entangled with this being."

"But you said it was a creature of intelligence beyond human comprehension. If it knows all and sees all, why does it need us?"

"Perhaps it knows enough to know it's incomplete. Or perhaps it became entwined with us by accident, and is now tied to us irrevocably."

"Well, I'm with you," I declared, pushing away the photos and Reader. "I don't want my life derailed by a lifetime of devotion to a weird ghost."

"The decision is entirely yours, but avoiding your fate may mean throwing your life away and beginning again." He put away the photos, but pushed the Reader back to me. "You might find that fighting it does no good. Read these books. In them, you'll see that every generation's servant writes that he is content, that he enjoys the company of the mysterious man he serves. I've always been wary of such unabashed compliance, but I was a cranky old man even when I was young." He tapped the Reader. "Once you read these stories, you'll know what to do. I can tell you're a smart kid."

I spent the better part of a day reading some of the stories, and none of them seemed so supernatural to me. Perhaps Uncle Jules had set my expectations too high, with a panicked warning about an eldritch beast, but I really didn't see what the big deal was. The stories weren't scary.

Then it was time to go back to school. I could not allow myself to be distracted from my studies by paranoia about some ethereal entity of incomprehensible blah-blah-blah. I powered through my final year much as I had all the others, with no romance, no frivolity, and no friends.

I was mere weeks away from taking the last portion of my medical exams, and filled with anxiety, as I had still not decided on whether to put my dexterity to use as a surgeon, or to indulge my love of puzzle-solving and go into internal medicine. I wished desperately for a sign.

And that was when my sleep, which had long been dreamless, was for the first time disturbed by a strange vision.

I should say, *eventually* it was a vision. But before any sight or sound, this dream was only a powerful feeling of being warm and safe. Cozy, I might go so far as to say, and yet I was somehow at the same time open and vulnerable and exposed – but I didn't mind that. Perhaps the best way to describe this unlikely combination of feelings was *belonging*. I knew, I simply knew that I was right where I was meant to be.

After basking in this unfamiliar but very welcome sensation for an indeterminate amount of time, it occurred to me that perhaps it could also be called "love." I had never been in love before, but this felt like I had always imagined it might feel: kind of warm, and exciting. It was like I was allowed to feel whatever I wanted to feel, and it would be good and right. As I let go, stopped analyzing and gave myself up to it, I was flooded with a tingling desire. I felt enamored, even though I hadn't the faintest idea who I was enamored with. I grew aroused, a physical sensation that I *was* familiar with, and that combined with the warm smitten feeling was so euphoric, so unlike anything I'd ever experienced – and yet at the same time it seemed like I'd waited my whole life for it.

This was when I began to see and hear, just a vague space and a comforting hum, but I wanted more of everything I was feeling, and I knew no other way to get it than to move in my new environment, to wiggle, and to seek it out.

My nebulous efforts were rewarded: I could feel myself becoming engulfed in voluptuous friction – inside and out. I began to moan with gratification even as I was growling with hunger for more. I squirmed and bounced and struggled to be completely conquered by this bliss.

I became so overwhelmed by this thing I felt that I was ready to die for it, to live for nothing else, and only then did I catch a glimpse of what – of *who* was providing these sensations. For a moment, it was a breath of smoke in the shape of a man, then it lost its shape and was only a wisp, and then it was a man again. The only thing about it that remained constant was a pair of piercing gray eyes, which glittered with mischief and held the knowledge of all the universe. But looking upon this ageless, faceless entity, I never felt anything but contentment. I surrendered myself to this veiled being, this all-seeing ghost, because I had never known such love, and I cared about nothing else. Inevitability tipped into a profound bliss, exploding inside me and carrying me into a sublime ecstasy.

I awoke in my familiar little room very disoriented. The suns had not yet risen, and so I was in darkness, at first only trying to recognize where I was, no more than that. Then, when I managed to turn the light on, I spent twenty minutes just trying to figure out if anything that I had been dreaming about had actually happened. I painstakingly put together what I had done last night, which was all the more difficult for it having been what I had done the night before, and the night before that: eat a bland meal, stare at a screen and study, and then fall asleep.

In comparison, the dream had been so vivid, so real and true and wonderful – but at the same time, I was unsettled by the things I had felt, by the pure, unconditional, and undeniably erotic love I had felt for that mysterious creature. There was no hope of falling back asleep, and so instead I sat up in bed and searched the room over and over for any sign of movement, of a presence. I thought that perhaps the dream was its way of telling me that it had found me – and this realization provoked a profound dread.

That was only the first dream. Several more followed, and each time, I awoke unsettled by the depth of love and joy I had felt for the elusive being who haunted me. Feeling so profoundly in sleep that there was nothing to be afraid of, being reassured so irresistibly that it was safe to relax into the sensation of being loved and cared for – it was deeply confusing. At first, it made me paranoid, and I spent every minute of the day searching the corners of my vision for the slightest trace of the entity. As the days passed, my waking hours became the nightmare, and the wonderful dreams my consolation – while I was having them. Others may have avoided sleep out of fear, but I found myself tempted to prolong it, to forego my waking life and seek the comfort of my dreams, where there was no conflict of feeling, just warmth and affection. It was only my years of self-enforced physical and mental discipline which gave me the wherewithal to resist.

But even I could not go on for very long, see-sawing between my blissful dreams and my waking fear of my fate, which now seemed terrifyingly inescapable. It was impossible to live this way, ever on the brink of succumbing to something I feared. I grew so anxious and confused and frustrated that I could not sit for my exams. I left school.

My mother was devastated, and I don't think she ever forgave me. It was months before she would speak to me. But it had been my last-ditch effort to save myself. The thing, the creature, only wanted someone who was a doctor. If I didn't become a doctor, surely I would be free of it?

But what if that was not enough to escape it? Perhaps I needed to continue on Uncle Jules' path, and travel as far away as I could. After all, he came out to the Yendar system, and then decades had gone by, and it had skipped over him.

Times were lean for a while as I planet-hopped. Work was hard to come by. Without my degree, I couldn't practice medicine, but I was ridiculously overqualified to do most other jobs. Once a potential employer found out that I had the level of education I had, they would refuse to hire me on the grounds that I would not find the work they had for me fulfilling. At last, I sought out a position in the military. I hated war, I feared death, but I had no other option.

Although I had not completed my residency or gotten licensed, the Orbital Defense Agency deemed me qualified to be a combat medic. Happy to be fed and paid, but still in fear of my ancestral fate, I submitted a request to be stationed in the most remote of outposts. I'll never forget the look on the face of the officer who looked over my history. A guy who narrowly missed a medical degree and who desperately wanted to get as far from civilization as he could? What must I have done? There was no way I could tell him the truth, it was too outlandish, and I could not come up with a convincing lie that would have made me look any better.

I was assigned to a garrison satellite, an artificial moon from which the ODA repelled pirates and other hostiles. It was not glamorous; it did not pay well; the food was atrocious, and we had the ugliest uniforms in all the colonies' numerous and sundry armed forces. But it was for the most part very boring, which was great. In a place this remote, a rough framework of military discipline stood strong, and so we all had to be out of bed early, lights-out was strictly enforced, and mealtimes were regimented, but once your maintenance and clean-up duties were taken care of, idleness was the only remaining order of the day. Most of my fellow soldiers organized team sports to pass the time, but that had never really been my thing. I wanted to catch up on all the books and movies I'd missed while I'd been at school. My mother and I were still not on good terms, but I appealed to a couple of my former classmates to transmit to me batches of things to read and watch.

The tenth or twelfth time the garrison went on alert, I decided I would first finish reading the last paragraph of the chapter I was on, as I was sure it was only another drill. Once I realized it was in fact an actual alert, I still was slow to move, because the couple of previous attacks had been so trivial: the pirates liked to buzz us once in a while, usually a tactic to keep a large portion of our forces occupied while one or two of their ships quietly raided a civilian cruiser in another part of the sector.

As I made for my battle-station, however, the bits and pieces I picked up on the way from my fellow soldiers, the urgent panic they expressed, told me this was something different. I was ordered by an officer to forego my usual station and head straight to the outer reaches of the base, where men were already in need of medical care.

This attack wasn't a diversion; the fleet of ships overhead and the irregular forces on the ground told me that today they were out to destroy the garrison. As I treated the injured men, sealing their wounds and loading them onto the hovering transports which took them back to the base, I glanced at the small craft that were landing and the men emerging from them, and determined that several rival groups had joined forces to obliterate this garrison, and probably others after it. Shortly after I came to this conclusion, a plasma bomb detonated nearby, and the last thing I saw was an enormous chunk of rock flying towards me and the man I was treating.

I awoke to find myself crammed into a bunk very similar to the bunk I was crammed into when I had first shipped out to the garrison, only now I was in agony, and my attempts to move were restricted by splints and bandaged grafts not yet healed. The man in the next bunk over told me where I was (on a transport to Dysa), our ultimate destination (the military hospital on that planet), and when the nurse would be by with more painkillers (not soon enough).

I survived the pirate invasion more or less intact, but my mobility and sanity had been sufficiently reduced that the ODA no longer had a use for me. I was discharged from the military hospital in one of Dysa's capital cities, and was promised a small monthly stipend for my troubles. The stipend would keep me barely fed and possibly semi-housed for the rest of my life, which was not the worst they could have done for me as thanks for my service, but it was hard to feel grateful.

I did not have enough money to get off the planet, and even if I had, I wasn't sure I'd be welcomed by anyone I knew, having made several stupid decisions which had ruined my career, compromised my health, and obliterated my independence. So I hung around Dysa, renting tiny rooms and eating in automated cafeterias, until I could hardly stand it anymore. I wanted a normal life. Perhaps becoming a doctor wouldn't have been the way to achieve that in the first place, but at least I would have had a real home, a secure future.

In an act of desperation, I went to the travel bureau to ask, semi-seriously, if indentured servitude was an option for getting off Dysa. As I sat waiting my turn to be seen at the counter, however, I heard my name called from a seat behind me. I turned. It was Loeb; he and

I had taken several classes together my first year of medical school, but after the third time he'd fainted during a dissection, he dropped out and studied chemical engineering instead. I hadn't seen him since.

Loeb changed seats to move closer to me. He asked all about how I was doing. He was there to book a trip back home, nothing special. I did not think that we had ever known each other well enough that I could depend on his charity, but I told him that if I didn't find a decent place to live on Dysa in approximately the next five minutes, I would need to take some sort of drastic measure.

"How do you feel about sharing a place?" he asked, and I shrugged. He told me, "I know a guy. Just let me get my trip booked and then I'll take you to him."

There was a research laboratory near the military hospital, and Loeb was kind enough to pay for my ticket for the shuttle over. "Now listen, this guy is kind of a weirdo. But he told me this morning that he had found this really nice place, except he couldn't afford by himself, and he couldn't find anyone to go in on it with him."

"Because he's a weirdo?"

"I think that's at least part of the reason, yeah."

The shuttle came to a halt, and we made for the exit. "If this place has got its own kitchen and bathroom," I said, "I can learn to live with a weirdo. If it's got a window, I can be especially tolerant."

Loeb took me down into the basement of the lab, where, as he had suspected, this acquaintance of his was still hunched over a computer, analyzing some compound or other. Loeb must have understood that a simple, cordial greeting would not be enough to shake him from his seat, so he announced, "I think I've found someone to room with you."

When standing at his full height, the guy towered over me. But he approached me with his hand held out, and I shook it. "How are you?" he said, and looked me up and down. "You have been in Alpha Garrison, I perceive." Then his gaze met mine, and his gray eyes glittered.

MAD SCIENTISTS NEED LOVE TOO

HELP WANTED, the notice said. *Must be good with computers. No experience necessary. To apply, simply express interest in the position aloud.* Paul read the notice over three times, in the hopes that it would start to make more sense. That did not work, but he remained intrigued. He met the only qualification specified in the notice, and he needed employment badly. All that was left to do was apply.

"I am interested in this job," he said to the empty room. A moment later, he felt suddenly and severely dizzy, and seemed to lose consciousness. When he regained his senses, he was standing on a floor made of metal grates, surrounded by complex machinery and blinking lights. Before him stood a reedy, angular man in a long white fitted coat with a high collar, buttoned on the left side rather than down the center. He wore elbow-length black rubber gloves and black boots, with a pair of black-rimmed goggles pushed up high on his forehead. His gray hair was receding slightly, but what remained was thick and lustrous. His blue eyes were piercing, and his bone structure severe, making him seem mostly cheekbone, balanced by jaw.

"Where am I?" Paul asked.

"You're in the laboratory aboard my spaceship," the man said. He invited Paul to look out of a nearby porthole, from which point Paul could see his home planet below.

"Did you teleport me here?" Paul asked, peering out.

"I did. I built a machine that detects the brainwave pattern of any person who read the particular combination of words in my notice, and then monitored those persons until they either stopped reading it or expressed an interest verbally, as you did. You'll have to forgive my methods, but I'm a wanted man, and it would be tricky for me to find an assistant in a more conventional way."

Locating an individual based on a specific brainwave pattern, from space? And then teleporting them instantly aboard a spaceship? "That's pretty impressive," Paul said.

The man smiled. "I'm glad you feel that way. I will be brief: My name is Doctor Eden Osmo, and I am a mad scientist seeking an assistant. The pay will be dismal, I'm afraid, but the position includes free room and board, and you get to travel the galaxy and do a lot of science."

Paul pondered this. "And if I were to say no — and I'm not saying no, I'm just asking, hypothetically — if I did, what would happen to me?"

"I'd wipe your memory and send you back home. You would have no idea you were ever gone."

"Oh, okay. I thought you might vaporize me, or use me in an experiment or something."

Osmo rolled his eyes. "I'm a *mad* scientist, not a *reckless* scientist. Kidnapping unemployed nerds willy-nilly isn't a good use of my time. In this business it's 'go big or go home,' quite frankly. So are you interested in the position?"

"Yeah, it sounds pretty interesting."

"Excellent. Can you operate this machine?" Osmo gestured towards a towering, complex computer whose monitor displayed a cryptic interface.

Paul walked over to it. "This is a Blackwell XR-338. I didn't get many opportunities on the 338 at the University, but I know my way around one."

"Then congratulations, you're hired. I'll teleport your things into your quarters, then set a course for our next destination. You'll have approximately six leisure hours between now and then."

Paul was sleeping off his teleportation-induced vertigo when Doctor Osmo summoned him to the laboratory. There, in the center of the room, was a three-dimensional holographic display of an oblate spheroid. The color patterns on it told Paul it was probably a planet.

"Are you ready for your first assignment?" Osmo asked, and without waiting for an answer, went on: "This is Phynos, the planet we are currently orbiting. Phynos was colonized about sixty years ago, mostly by miners who are slowly extracting the planet's mineral resources. The thing is, I need one of those resources, a lot of it, and very quickly, to build my indestructible robot army."

Now the holographic display was showing a boxy metal device with spindly legs. Zooming out, it became apparent that this device was one of hundreds, which spread out evenly to surround the planet in orbit. Glowing red lines connected each device to its neighbors.

"I have built this extraction system, which will unearth the necessary materials and collect them using tractor beams. It's pretty ingenious, if I do say so myself. Once the devices are orbiting the planet, no additional energy source is necessary. The gravitational force of the planet itself powers their extraction. All that's left is to program this system to extract only what I want, and that is krytanium. I'd very much like to focus on the designs for the robots I'll then be able to build, so I'm assigning the programming of the extraction devices to you."

"Sounds easy," Paul said, *possibly* lying.

"I'll leave you to it, then. Notify me when the devices are ready to be implemented."

Paul sat down at the XR-338's terminal and got right to work. With a little research, he found the composition of the mineral Osmo wanted, and instructed the extraction devices to only collect materials that had that precise atomic composition, not a proton more or an electron less. When he had been at it for nine or ten hours, his eyes dry and his head fuzzy, he wondered how he was supposed to clock out. Should he wait to be dismissed for the day?

He pressed the intercom button, and Osmo promptly answered, "Yes, what is it?"

"Would it be alright if I took a break?"

"Of course you can! I create monsters; I'm not a monster myself. Nefarious deeds are best carried out when one is fed and well-rested. See you tomorrow."

Paul stared at the intercom speaker for a few seconds more after Osmo clicked off. He was glad to hear what he'd heard, but Osmo's assertion seemed almost as kind as it was pragmatic. Osmo wasn't really following the model of the mad scientists Paul was familiar with, but then again, this wasn't the movies. Paul shrugged at no one, turned away from the intercom, and went to find some food.

All in all, being a mad scientist's assistant was a pretty good deal. Paul had everything he needed; he got to use an XR-338 all day long, and no one bothered him while he was working. Who could ask for more?

Paul didn't even see Doctor Osmo for the last two days of the extraction programming project. Once he had everything figured out, his boss was happy to let him work independently. Only when he had successfully compiled the code did Paul click the intercom again and let Osmo know that the plan was ready to proceed.

Sitting at his master control board, Osmo navigated the extraction devices into position around the planet. Paul stood behind him and watched on the big viewscreen. When Osmo flipped the switch, red beams of light shot from one device to another, just like they had in the holographic simulation. The surface of the planet began to tremble, and Osmo yelped joyously, "*Yesss!* It's working! Soon I will have my robot army, and with them I will—"

As the planet began to crumble and warp, Osmo fell silent. His hundreds of devices were collecting huge chunks of material, so quickly and plentifully that the planet was beginning to collapse.

"That's not right," Osmo muttered. "There was not nearly that much krytanium in Phynos. What is happening?"

Paul's eyes got wide. "Sorry, did you say 'krytanium'?"

"Yes, I did. Why is that a surprise to you?" Osmo leapt from his chair and grabbed Paul by the collar. "What did you do?"

"I thought you said *tri*tanium!" Paul gasped, as he was lifted bodily by a surprisingly powerful Osmo. "I programmed the devices to extract the tritanium!"

"You fool! The planet can't sustain the extraction of the tritanium, there's too much of it!"

Both men watched helplessly as the planet collapsed into millions of fragments, dispersing and floating through space. Some of these rocks collided with the extraction devices, crushing them utterly. Much of this debris was doubtless the krytanium that Osmo so desperately coveted, but with no planet to generate a magnetic field, there was no device capable of collecting it effectively.

"I'm sure we can recover some of the extractors," Paul said. "And then you'll have lots of tritanium. That's got to count for something, right?"

"You can't build robots out of tritanium! You can't build *anything* out of it!" Osmo collapsed into his chair, head in hands, weeping unabashedly.

Paul wrung his hands. "I guess this means I'm out of a job...?"

Osmo lifted his face from his hands, slowly stood up, and stalked over to Paul. He drew close enough that Paul cowered under Osmo's towering figure, and looked at the ground.

"Look at me," Osmo commanded.

Paul forced his chin upwards, his eyes darting to meet Osmo's for an instant, before shying away again.

"I said look at me!" Osmo's breath was hot on Paul's cheek. Paul met Osmo's gaze again, and held it this time.

Abruptly, Osmo spun on his heels and walked away, back toward the viewscreen. "No, you're not out of a job. For two reasons." Here he dramatically held up two fingers, and then just one, as he said, "First! Because that's what you want most in the universe right now: to be fired, so you cannot be here, facing my wrath. Keeping you on as my assistant will be a delicious punishment. But second!" Osmo held two fingers up again, then turned back, clasping his hands behind his back and barreling in Paul's direction once more. "I have never seen a person as terrified as you are right now, and I have seen many terrified people. If there's one thing I can be sure of in this moment, it is that you will never, *ever* make a mistake like this again. I just paid heavily for this lesson, and being so invested, the most worthwhile thing for me would be to continue to employ you — you, who have just acquired a lot of wisdom that cannot be gained from books or drills."

Paul gulped, and nodded.

"Now, I'm afraid there's no time to collect the remaining extractors and their useless cargo of tritanium. A planetary catastrophe like this will summon every governmental and law enforcement authority from around the galaxy, and those that possess faster-than-light capabilities will be here in minutes. We must leave now. But I can fly the ship myself, so you are dismissed. I will summon you when I have a new task for you."

Paul was careful to avoid Osmo after that, for fear of further incurring his wrath. He stayed in his quarters when Osmo was milling about the ship, spending a lot of time, at first, dwelling on the mistake he'd made, replaying the disaster in his head. He thought about all the poor miners that had been on the planet, and it occurred to him: assuming that one used Osmo's extraction network correctly, it would actually save a lot of trouble, a lot of hard labor, if mining companies used the machines instead of sending people to pull resources out of the ground manually. It was too bad Osmo seemed so determined to be a mad scientist, or else Paul might suggest this alternative method of application to him. If nothing else, licensing it would be a great way to make money. But he assumed that Osmo was not interested in any idea he had at the moment. Only when he was sure Osmo was sleeping did Paul leave his quarters; at those times, he did a lot of exploring, familiarizing himself with the other equipment in the laboratory, as well as Osmo's extensive library and the smaller workshops he had set up in every spare corner. He was perusing a book on quantum teleportation when Osmo's voice boomed over the intercom, demanding his presence in front of the XR-338 immediately.

"I wrote this program months ago. I need you to debug it." Osmo briefly explained the purpose of the program, then turned to leave. "I have other business to deal with. I'm sure you'll do fine."

Sure I'll do fine? Paul thought. After what happened? But Osmo had been right when he'd said that Paul would be too afraid to make a mistake this time.

It didn't take him long to discover just how much debugging Osmo's code needed. Paul could tell by the nature of the mistakes that Osmo was a competent programmer, and given enough time, he could have perfected this code himself. The errors were nearly all due to finger-slips and forgetfulness, Paul had no doubt. But the sheer number of them made the task a major endeavor.

With no natural light or clocks to guide his behavior, Paul's sleep schedule began to drift. He simply worked until he was tired, slept until he woke, and ate when he was hungry. And so when he found himself by chance eating at the little table in the kitchen with Osmo sitting across from him, it could have been three days since he'd begun the debugging, or four.

Osmo's slow but rhythmic motions — fork to food, food to mouth — were interrupted just long enough for him to ask, "How are things coming along?"

"I'm working it out," Paul replied, after a thoughtful pause.

"The code was a mess, you can say it." Osmo poked at his food. "I was in a rush just to get it written, you know, get it out. But when it came time to debug it, I lost interest, got distracted." Paul watched as Osmo raised his head only to stare into the middle distance, his eyes intense as always but now with an added touch of melancholy. "That happens sometimes."

Then, seeming to have realized that he was lost in an embarrassing reverie, Osmo straightened up, squared his shoulders, and cleared his throat. "But that's what I have you for, is it not? To do all the drudge work." He forced a little smile at this. Paul assumed that Osmo meant for it to look like a cruel grin, but his heart wasn't in it.

"Indeed," said Paul, unable to come up with a better response.

When Paul got the code to compile, he did not inform Osmo right away. He thought it might be better to test the program on a small scale first, so that he could be sure that what he presented to Osmo was functional and effective. He was sure Osmo would not miss just one little mouse, and just one little proton pistol, if he only borrowed them for a few minutes.

Once Paul was sure that his experiment was a success, he tracked down Osmo in the library. "Are we near any inhabited worlds?" he asked.

Osmo's expression brightened as it dawned on him what Paul's question implied. "Is it ready?" he replied, and Paul had barely begun to nod in reply before Osmo had grabbed him by the arm to drag him to the master control board.

Osmo had cloaked the ship and tucked it away on the dark side of a satellite orbiting a planet with a Level Zero civilization, and so it took him only a few minutes to position the ship where his new weapon would be effective. He loaded the new program into the control terminal, focused his all-purpose beam weapon, and used his ultrascope to target an unsuspecting sapient being on the planet's surface.

Osmo's target, who was sitting outside, having a conversation with someone else, did not seem to be affected by the beam. He did not hesitate or twitch in the slightest. Paul did not know how, from this great a distance, they would be able to test whether the weapon was effective. But then Osmo, rifling through a nearby storage compartment, came up with an elaborate joystick, only partially secured in a case, wires still sprouting from the core of its machinery.

Paul watched through the ultrascope as Osmo manipulated the joystick...and then their target raised one hand and slapped himself across the face.

"It works! Ha ha!" Osmo stamped his feet with excitement. "Would you like to have a go?"

"Really?" Paul put his hand over his heart.

"You earned it, for certain."

Osmo handed the joystick over, their fingers brushing as Paul took it up. He played around for a while, until he could get their target to stand up and jump into a nearby fountain. The being's companion was in a hilarious panic. Osmo and Paul shared a lengthy laugh at the expense of both, until Osmo collapsed into his chair, and Paul had to lean on the console to get his bearings. As their laughter faded, their eyes met, and for the first time, Paul saw true joy in them. Surely this meant that he had won Osmo's approval, that he might even be forgiven for his accidental destruction of that mining planet.

One thing was for sure, Paul wanted to maintain the momentum. He wanted to do something fun together, to feel closer to Osmo. "Who shall we target next? How are we going to use this thing?"

Osmo looked down at the joystick in his hand. "To be honest, I had always been so far away from any hope of completing the Mind Control Beam, I hadn't bothered to put a lot of thought into who I might use it on." He set the joystick down. "I'll work on that."

Osmo's lack of enthusiasm about using such a powerful weapon as the Mind Control Beam was confusing to Paul. It occurred to him that perhaps his blunder with the extraction web had made Osmo hesitant to use any other devices, in case Paul inadvertently sabotaged them again.

But if that were the case, why would Osmo invite him to help with yet another project, this one being a machine that controlled the weather?

"This is something I haven't built yet," Osmo said, as he laid out some sketches and handwritten notes. "You're very bright, and I know that you've been doing some reading in my library, so perhaps you and I together can come up with the most effective method by which we could generate artificial weather conditions."

Osmo had spent considerable time studying the properties and behaviors of planetary ionospheres, and when Paul examined Osmo's notes, he came up with a few vague ideas about manipulating that atmospheric layer.

"We could use electromagnetic frequencies to direct pulsing energy beams into the planet's ionosphere, to heat it up, to excite it." Paul's face grew hot when he said some of these words out loud. Osmo looked up from the papers to give Paul a brief, knowing look, which perhaps was meant to scold him for being immature, but at the same time hinted that he might have found that combination of phrases amusing as well.

Paul and Osmo worked together for several weeks, scribbling out designs and trading ideas. Occasionally, something that one of them had said would remind Osmo of an interesting story, and Osmo would relate it to Paul; it usually involved someone who had wronged him at some University, and how he had exacted his revenge. Paul didn't have any stories quite like that, but he had an epic prank or two under his belt, and would in turn tell Osmo about the mischief he'd got up to in his school days, such as the summer he spent dressing up as a rival student and distributing bird seed all alone on the campus quad, gradually training the pigeons who frequented the campus, until the first day of the fall quarter, when that kid walked out onto the quad and was immediately mobbed by a hundred pigeons. Osmo betrayed only the slightest amusement at first, but after another story, about he and his buddies getting onto the roofs of elevators and scaring the daylights of anyone who happened to want to ride them in the more conventional way, Paul did get a genuine laugh out of him, and was terrifically proud.

Sometimes, Osmo would go off on a tangent about his dreams for the weather machine, how he would use it to create hurricanes and hailstorms until his victims paid him handsomely to turn his machine off, and Paul didn't have a lot to add to that, so he would just take the opportunity to gaze at Osmo, his high cheekbones, his stern mouth, his bright eyes, the thinnest of dignified mannerisms that veiled his wrathful outbursts.

The longer they worked together, the more in sync they became, anticipating each other's movements so that they did not bump into each other while working at the drafting table, and anticipating each other's thoughts as well, weaving them into a seamless design. Sadly, once they had drawn up a set of blueprints, Osmo was certain that his all-purpose beam weapon was not powerful enough to accommodate a weather-manipulation function, and he did not have on his ship even half the materials necessary to build something suitable. "It will take a long time, a lot of planet-hopping, and a lot of clandestine searching to get this instrument built," he lamented. "But that's alright, there's plenty of things to do in the meantime. How about a cup of coffee?"

They sat in front of the viewscreen, watching the stars wheel past while they had their coffee. Paul thought he was the only one purposely drinking slowly to extend this quiet time together, but when Osmo set his cup down, Paul could see that Osmo had barely sipped more than he himself had.

Osmo cleared his throat. "Paul, I just want to say how very nice it's been having you as my assistant. I hadn't realized, until you arrived, just how dull it was being a mad scientist. Oh, I had my little schemes here and there, but I just couldn't stick to anything, you know? Couldn't get motivated to follow through. And who could blame me, really? I mean, what's it all for, being lonely and bent on world domination? At the end of it all, I would still be lonely, wouldn't I?"

Paul looked intently at Osmo, hoping desperately for Osmo to look back, to meet his eyes. "I would imagine knowing that would be kind of demoralizing, yes."

"But you've changed everything. It's not just having someone around. I've had people around before. But there's something different about you, something I wouldn't want to ever do without again."

Osmo did not look Paul in the eye, but his gaze did travel to Paul's mouth, which opened slightly in anticipation. Osmo leaned in a fraction, before stopping himself. "Oh, but I must seem like such an old man to you."

"That's okay, I like older men," Paul said, then immediately clapped his hand over his mouth, his face heating up beneath it. He hastened to say instead, "I mean to say that I like you, too, Doctor, just as you are."

Osmo smiled fondly at Paul. "Spending time with you these past few weeks, I feel more invigorated than I ever have, but you've made all my resentment and vengefulness seem very...silly I'm not sure that I want to go on as the person I was."

"Do you mean you don't want to be a mad scientist anymore?"

"I want to know what your ideas are," he said. "I think we might be able to accomplish more if we carried on as...partners. What would *you* like us to do?"

"We could be mad scientists together. I think I would be okay with that." Paul wasn't sure if what he wanted to say was what Osmo wanted to hear, but he said it anyway: "What if we were *good* scientists instead, though? Take that weather machine, for example. What if instead of terrorizing people with bad weather to get a ransom, we found places that were in need of rain, like farmers for example, and gave them some? We'd probably get a nice reward from them anyway, they'd be so thankful for our help." The way Osmo looked at him, intensely, with brow furrowed, Paul was sure he'd just made a mistake. But then Osmo said, "Go on."

Paul scrambled to articulate the thoughts he'd had about the beneficial uses for the extraction — including the profitability of it.

Osmo stroked his chin as he pondered this. "That just might work. Very well." He looked at Paul, his eyes gleaming with excitement. "I knew all along. There was something about you, I knew you had something in you. I feel a new sense of purpose, and I owe it to you. Tomorrow we shall begin brainstorming ways we might use my existing machines for good." Osmo placed one gloved hand on Paul's knee. "I say tomorrow, because I am wondering if tonight, you might accompany me to my quarters...?"

Paul was unsure of how to proceed; he assumed that some seduction would be in order, but he didn't feel very seductive himself, just generally as a person. That left Osmo, and although at first Paul assumed Osmo's assertiveness would make him a natural at seduction, looking back, what Osmo demonstrated more than anything was gruff annoyance. That was not a good indicator of seduction capabilities...was it?

In any case, Paul was, to sum up, utterly uncertain as to which of them should start undressing the other, as they stood facing each other in Osmo's dim, sparsely-decorated quarters. Ultimately, he decided that with fifteen buttons across and down Osmo's white lab coat, they would probably do best to make undoing them a team effort, so he volunteered to start.

To Paul's confusion, Osmo did not join in. At first he lifted one hand, but then dropped it again. Instead, he watched Paul work, and Paul felt self-conscious about how long he was taking, his fingers fumbling. He laughed. "It's just, there's so many buttons," he said. "And I did not wake up today anticipating that I would be doing, uh this, with you."

"Nor I."

"Sorry, I feel like this is supposed to be more...frantic? Passionate? It seems like in the movies and television, when people are doing it for the first time, someone's always got to sweep everything off the nearest flat surface and flop onto it because they just can't wait a minute longer. Has that been your experience?"

With all the buttons undone at last, Osmo shrugged out of the coat, folding it neatly over the back of a chair. "I haven't had a lot of experience at this," he admitted. "Being a mad scientist takes up a lot of one's time."

Paul bit his lip. "That's okay. I don't have a lot of experience either."

"We shouldn't have said anything," Osmo sighed. "Then neither of us would have known that the other had no idea what he was doing. But in any case, I can tell you that I would not appreciate having everything swept off any surface in this ship...it may not seem organized, but I assure you I know where everything is."

"Luckily for us, there's a bed right here," Paul said. He cringed a little at having said this – it wasn't exactly a smooth suggestion. But Osmo did not seem to mind it. He sat on the edge of the bed to unlace his boots. He toed them off, and when he looked up at Paul, Paul's stomach dropped. It was something about how Osmo looked, with all his mad scientist accoutrements gone. The coat and boots, the gloves and goggles, they made him look impressive, but only for looking at. Now, in just a plain shirt and slacks and stocking feet, he looked... well, Paul would hesitate to use the word "normal," and the word "accessible" also seemed inappropriate. But "touchable" would do nicely. The excitement that had seemed strangely absent a few minutes ago now flooded Paul's veins.

The fabric of Osmo's shirt was so thin, Paul could discern the peaks of his nipples through it. Paul stepped close enough to place his hand on Osmo's chest, flicking over one nipple with just the tip of his little finger. Osmo drew in a breath and quickly let it out with a soft vocalization. Overcome with lust, Paul pushed Osmo, encouraging him to lay back on the bed. Osmo started to comply, but he stopped himself abruptly and hauled himself upright, turning to look at the rest of the bed. It was easily big enough for two, but aside from the narrow edge they were sitting on, where he slept, the whole thing was covered in technical manuals, blueprints, journals, and scribbled-on scraps.

"Sorry about all this," Osmo said, hastily gathering the mess up. "Who doesn't like a little light reading before bed, hm?"

Paul tried to help, sifting through and stacking the papers. "Or a little light scheming...or *heavy* scheming, wow. Did you do all these doodles of people screaming in terror?"

"Those are *diagrams*."

"They're good. You ever think about being an artist?"

Osmo rolled his eyes. "I'm not that kind of crazy."

With the bed cleared they could stretch out, bending and unfolding their limbs as they undressed each other. Paul petted the salt-and-pepper hair on Osmo's chest while Osmo worked free the buttons of Paul's jeans.

It wasn't long after they had their clothes off, though, before Osmo remarked, "It's chilly in here, isn't it? Sorry about that." He crawled under the blankets, encouraging Paul to join him. They folded their arms around each other, seeking the comfort of a lover's clinch.

Osmo was so soft and warm, much more so than his icy eyes could ever hint at. Paul thought it somewhat of a shame that Osmo's body was now mostly concealed from his sight, almost as quickly as it had been revealed to him; then again, now he had an excuse to learn him by feel, and he did so with enthusiasm, running his fingers boldly down the length of Osmo's spine and across his flank. Osmo was more tentative, but his fingers would tighten on Paul's shoulder or hip whenever Paul did something he especially appreciated.

The most delicious feeling of all, though, was the way their plump erections pressed between their bellies. They were so close together now, rubbing against each other, that they were breathing into each other's mouths, and Paul closed that final distance with a kiss. They mashed their mouths together, the hot, wet contact making Paul's stomach flip. His tongue sipped in and out of Osmo's mouth, mimicking actions he might like to undertake with other parts of himself. Each time their mouths met anew, he could feel their pricks jerk and throb in sync.

The head of Osmo's cock would occasionally catch at Paul's belly button, but it was slick, now, and each time slid right out and along. Rubbing their pricks against each other was inelegant and imprecise, but it left Paul's hand free to wander, gliding along anything that was hard and flat and cupping anything that was soft and round.

As he roamed, Paul's wrist brushed the tip of Osmo's cock, touching the wetness there. Paul placed the pad of his middle finger against the slit, rubbing gently up and down. Osmo's hips began to rock, seeking more contact. But as this happened under the covers, all Paul saw was Osmo's eyes sliding shut and his mouth falling open as he softly exhaled. Rather than grab Paul's hand and make him stroke the way he wanted, Osmo wrapped his own hand around Paul's cock, gripping firmly but stroking slowly. Paul had a lot of foreskin, so even though he was fully erect, Osmo could rub and slide it with his palm all over and around the sensitive glans and crown. Paul instinctively held Osmo's cock more tightly, as if to secure himself as things began to accelerate.

Then Paul got an idea. He shifted his hips so he could attempt to enclose Osmo's cock alongside his own in a single grip, pressing the sensitive undersides more tightly together. His hand wasn't quite large enough, but Osmo clasped his own hand around them, and that did the trick. They both pumped into this tight, hot confinement. Their foreskins did most of the work, letting them slide deliciously back and forth as the wetness of their pre-come increased and the friction diminished.

Their tugging and frotting didn't feel like quite enough, but Paul didn't want to pause, and Osmo didn't seem to, either – to attempt anything more would require stopping what they were doing. Their mutual pleasure was not quite reaching the level of "fervor" but it was definitely in the territory of "eager," or perhaps "rollicking." But the crush of bodies, the motions of sex, and the smell of each other's skin as they sweated with their exertions pulled them into a spiral of ecstasy that found its pinnacle when Paul cried out, "Oh Doctor, I—" and began to climax, making everything slippery and hot beneath the covers. Osmo was only an instant behind, and they worked each other through it, their rhythm reduced to erratic shudders. Then, their soft sighs of gratification mingled as they calmed in each other's arms.

The room didn't seem so cold now, and Paul pushed the covers away. He then did his best to roll just far enough to one side to grab his shirt off the floor without smearing the mess everywhere, and used the shirt to tidy things as best he could. Anything more thorough would have required getting out of bed, and he just wasn't interested in that. He idly stroked Osmo's chest and belly, and murmured, "That was fun."

He tilted his head up, expecting Osmo to concur. Osmo's expression was not disagreeable, but it hinted that he had not thought about fun in several years. "Yes, I suppose it was," he said, and when his gaze met Paul's, they could only smile at each other for a moment before looking away, bashful again.

Paul woke in the middle of the night. He looked over and found Osmo deeply asleep. Moving slowly, he climbed out of bed and made his way to the kitchen for a glass of water. On his way back, he had a new idea, and made a detour to the master control board.

Paul had never operated the all-purpose beam weapon by himself, but he'd watched Osmo a few times, and it had seemed pretty intuitive. He examined the dial, and turned it until it read "SCORCH."

The ship was orbiting an uninhabited planet; they had been watching its weather patterns while they fine-tuned a few ideas about atmospheric manipulation. Paul pointed the ultrascope at a wide, arid patch of land, then looked through it, seeing nothing but dirt, a few dry trees, and some rocks. Paul pointed the beam at this brown patch of land and flicked it on. The beam hit a tree, vaporizing it instantly. Paul quickly switched off the beam, and examined the charcoal remains.

"Oops," he whispered.

He tried again, this time pointing the beam at the most featureless area he could locate, and when he turned the beam on, he kept it on, gently moving it, guiding its burning path, a curve here, a few short strokes there. When he was satisfied with the job he'd done, he powered the console down and returned to bed.

The next morning, Paul led Osmo to the control room, and invited him to look at the viewscreen. There, Osmo saw what Paul had drawn: burnt into the desert, a hundred miles wide, was a heart. An arrow pierced the heart, and inside it had been drawn the initials **P.H.** and **E.O.**

SOFT AND STICKY

ALEC FOUGHT the urge to clutch at Trace's sleeve or belt as they moved through the bustling crowd. It wasn't that he was afraid – he was never *afraid*, and anyway it was only a bazaar. But with the way Trace was zig-zagging confidently through the crush of people, knowing exactly where he was going, Alec was afraid of losing him. Trying to stay close without touching Trace, Alec instead kept stepping on his heels, and apologizing.

The stall that Trace stopped in front of seemed no different than any other: a striped canopy shielded its proprietor, Tulip, from the midday sun, and the merchandise was packed tightly into woven baskets.

"Trace!" Tulip flung all four arms out at the sight of him. "My most beloved customer!"

"I'll bet you say that to anyone who's got money to burn," Trace shot back with a grin.

"I do this, yes," Tulip admitted, "but only with you do I mean it in truth! Now, in what can I interest you today?"

Trace pretended to survey Tulip's goods, knowing full well that what he was looking for was not out and visible. "Something a little more unusual than this," he said at last, making a small gesture to indicate Tulips's baskets.

Tulip looked at Trace's face, then past him, at Alec, who was peering over his shoulder at all of the oddly-shaped and brightly-colored fruits that Tulip had on display. "I think I know what you mean, yes?" Tulip said, and nodded subtly towards Alec. "Something better enjoyed by two, you are looking for. You have not been by for that in a long time."

"Yeah, well, I've had other things going on," Trace shrugged.

"Congratulations, then, I say to you, because you are in luck: I have one, and you have a reason to ask for one. We are both fortunate." Tulip bent down behind the baskets, rummaging in a box at his feet. He came up with a plain, rough sack, which he held up with one hand, waiting for Trace to put a tall stack of coins in the open palm of another. "My friend, my friend, and my favorite customer," Tulip chirped as he dropped the bag into Trace's hands. "You know it will be worth every credit."

Trace and Tulip both touched their fingers to their foreheads, the cordial farewell of Tulip's people. As Trace turned to lead the way back through the bazaar, he handed Alec the sack. Alec immediately untied it to see what was inside, but Trace clasped his hands over the bundle. "Don't!"

"I just wanted to see what it was," Alec sulked. "You've been very mysterious about it all day."

"I'll tell you what it is when we get back to the ship. For now, just don't let anyone see what you've got, and don't touch it with your bare hands."

This only intrigued Alec further. "Is it dangerous?" he said, far more eager than anxious.

Trace tried to keep his mouth close to Alec's ear as they wove through the crowd. "It is if anyone sees we have one. They are exceedingly rare, and you don't find them unless you know a guy like I know a guy."

"Are they illegal?"

"Only in sixteen systems. The sixteen that know they exist. But listen, what have I told you? What's the most important thing?"

Alec sifted through the various tidbits of wisdom that Trace had imparted to him, trying to think of the one most appropriate to this situation. He ventured, "That nothing's illegal so long as you don't get caught?"

"Very good. There just might be some hope for you yet, in this racket."

Trace had worked very hard and waited very patiently for this day. He had paid off all his debts, fulfilled all his obligations, and then taken advantage of that brief window of time, after a new base of operations had been established but before the Red Faction's scouts had the opportunity to sniff it out. Those were always days of hard work, scrambling to get as much accomplished as possible before it was time to focus on combat again, but the quiet nights made it worth it. The trip to the bazaar had been the final step in months of planning, and now it was time for the culmination.

As the door to Trace's quarters slid shut behind him, he closed his eyes and said a small silent prayer, in the hopes of warding off interruptions. Alec was sitting on the bed, watching Trace walk around it to join him, having very little idea of what was about to happen.

From beneath the bed, Trace dragged a locked metal box. Inside was the sack containing his recent purchase. He placed it on the bed.

"You won't want this staining your clothes," he muttered.

"Better get undressed, then, huh?" Alec said, in a sly way, as though the evening was taking a naughty turn that was completely unexpected, rather than meticulously planned.

Trace moved to pull his own shirt off, but he was interrupted by Alec's hands. Alec insisted that they get undressed the way *he* liked; that is, they would do it to each other, and there would be some playful tickling integrated into it. Trace tolerated the tickling, and was more amenable to the part where Alec eagerly tugged his clothes off of him.

Being utterly naked was a rare occurrence, as vigilance was the price of being part of the Splinter Faction, and it was inadvisable to be caught in the middle of a raid undressed and unarmed. It was a pity, Trace mused, that being naked with Alec was an almost unthinkable luxury, when it ought to have been a daily occurrence. But he could not let his regret spoil that luxury when it did arrive. He reached into the sack and pulled from it a plump, glossy red fruit. It filled his hand, his fingers spread across its smooth curves.

Alec was immediately riveted to the sight of it. Perhaps it was all the suspense that had surrounded this moment, but Alec couldn't take his eyes off the fruit. Something about its shape and color looked so inviting, so *enticing*, in a way that no food ever had before – even though he wasn't hungry at all. "Can I touch it?" he breathed.

"I want you to," Trace said, and placed the fruit into Alec's cupped hands. The skin of it was velvety soft, seemingly firm but supple, giving gently under even the delicate press of Alec's fingers. It felt like it was overfull inside, and near ready to burst right in his hand.

Trace pointed to the subtle crease that ran the length of it. "What you want to do is run your thumb right along here." Following Trace's instructions, Alec pressed the pad of his thumb into the cleft, sliding it up and down. "That's good," Trace said, "just like that."

With a few more strokes, the delicate skin of the fruit opened up, and thick crimson juice began to ooze out and over Alec's thumb. "Oh," Alec said.

Trace leaned down and took Alec's thumb into his mouth, sucking the juice away. "Perfect. Oh, it's perfectly ripe. I knew Tulip wouldn't let me down."

Trace nudged Alec's hands, encouraging him to hold the fruit close to his lips and lick away the fresh juice that had seeped to the surface. Alec opened his mouth and touched the cleft of the fruit with just the tip of his tongue, sliding it along the length, gathering up every drop. It was sweet and tangy, but with something more, something so delicious that it made Alec groan. He ran the flat of his tongue along the seam again, squeezing the fruit, eager to taste every single drop of its glistening juice.

"Good, isn't it?" Trace said. "But don't hurry. We're not going to have another one of these for a long time, so we've got to savor it.

Here, let me." Trace slowly took the fruit from Alec's clutching hands. He pressed both thumbs against the cleft and then inward, rubbing the skin there to open it wider, and when a fresh burst of thick, sticky juice gushed out, he tilted Alec's chin up with one hand, and let the juice flow into his open mouth, over his eager, pouting lips.

Alec licked at every drop that spilled across his lips, moaning at the rich sweetness and the subtle but invigorating tingle that the juice provoked wherever it touched his skin. A few drops went astray, trickling over his collarbones and down his chest. He looked down at them, but before he could move to scoop them up with his fingers, Trace said, "Don't. We'll get it later."

Alec was feeling just the slightest bit light-headed now, not unlike how he felt when his cock was hard and had gone untouched for too long. In fact, now that he was looking down, he saw that his erection was rock-hard and ramrod-straight; he'd been so enthralled by the taste of the fruit, he hadn't even noticed any sensation happening lower than his mouth.

Meanwhile, Trace was pouring what seemed to be the last of the juice into his own mouth. Alec looked on with jealousy, wanting it for himself, but at the same time, he felt certain that he would never experience anything so erotic as the sight of Trace with his head thrown back and juice trickling down his jaw and neck, and he wanted to watch it forever.

Trace tilted his head forward only when the last drops had fallen over his lips. Then, digging both thumbs into the open cleft of the fruit, he pulled until he split it in half, exposing the dense, glistening flesh inside. He handed one half to Alec.

"Do I just bite it?" Alec asked.

"You bite, you lick, you do whatever you want. But *slowly*."

Alec contemplated his half for a moment, then had an idea. He grasped Trace's hand, the one that had his piece of the fruit in it, and took a bite; then, before Trace could protest, he offered Trace a bite of his own piece. Trace smiled when he understood, and pulled Alec close with his free arm, licking away the juice on Alec's fingers after sinking his teeth into the fruit's thick flesh.

As they fed each other, the fruit gave up more juice, which dribbled down their bodies, pearly-red drops staining their arms and their bellies and their thighs and their cocks. Having reached a plateau of pleasure, they nibbled at the fruit as though in a trance, languidly, dazzled by the taste of the pulpy fruit and the heat of their skin where they were pressed against each other. Pursing their lips to suck away the juice from each bite of fruit and from their dripping hands, they slurped and moaned and devoured every morsel, their hot breath in each other's palms, their tongues between each other's fingers.

When one tiny bite remained, both eyed it, but at last Trace pressed it to Alec's lips. The moment Alec took it into his mouth, Trace's tongue followed, tasting the last sweet remnants as he deeply explored Alec's teeth and gums and tongue.

Now, all that was left to satisfy their craving was the errant juice that had splashed all over their flushed bodies. Alec was panting, still desperate but certain that he'd be satisfied if he could have just a *little* more. He ducked his head down and slid his tongue all across Trace's collarbones and chest, teasing his nipples, in search of a drop here, another there.

When he had lapped up all he could reach there, Trace gripped his shoulder and guided him to the bed, facing him but oriented in the other direction, so that each of them could gather up the remaining juice from the other's body, lower and lower. Tongues dipped into navels, lips pressed against the tender skin just below, licking juice from the crest of a hip bone, the join of a thigh. Muscles twitched and flexed beneath hot, wet mouths, desire coursing madly through their veins.

In their lustful haze, not bothering with the playful teasing with which they usually delighted one another, they laved each other's cocks, tongues fully extended to gather every precious lingering taste of tangy sweetness. Even when all that was left was the taste in their mouths, their frenzied passion had barely dissipated, and they continued to suckle, their pulsing, glistening cocks as red and plump as the fruit had been. Their mutual pleasure spiraled higher, wet and messy, until they provoked in each other one final burst of ecstasy, and one last gushing mouthful.

Only now did they feel sated, their damp limbs splayed, their heaving chests slowly calming. Trace rolled onto his back, and Alec rested his head on Trace's thigh, one arm wrapped around his hip, feeling unsteady even though he was stretched out, still and safe, on the bed.

"I can see why those things are illegal," Alec said. "If I could, I'd eat one every day, and I imagine I would never get anything done. If everyone did that, whole societies would collapse."

"Yeah, that would probably be a bad thing. But you do get to enjoy *me* every day, and that's been a good thing so far, right?"

Alec lifted his head to grin at Trace, then hauled himself up so that he might climb up Trace's body, until they could share a kiss. "It's somewhat of a consolation," he said, with his forehead pressed to Trace's, and even without the fruit's invigorating influence, they soon gathered the energy to enjoy each other once more.

AND THEN THERE WAS THE ONE ABOUT...

THE JADED TRAVELER

AMID WAS FINALLY ready to admit that he had become jaded. A lifetime spent planet-hopping, charming sentient beings of every shape and size, experiencing every pleasurable sensory experience the galaxy had to offer, had made it difficult to for him these days to get a thrill out of anything at all. And he needed thrills. He needed them to survive, or at least it seemed so to him.

Wandering through the largest, most varied "entertainment district" on Ku Pirr, barely dazzled by the blinking, flashing signs which lured patrons in with the promise of the simplest of sex acts, Amid's eye was caught by a discreet sign on a plain door, an etched metal plate which read *Unique Experiences For The Cultivated And Discerning.*

There was no guard, no password; Amid walked right in, and found himself in a cozy, elegantly furnished lobby. The host, a Ku Pirrian, sat behind a desk opposite the door.

"Welcome," the host said to him. "Are you interested in our services today?"

"I am," Amid said. "I am definitely in need of something unique."

The host, probably accustomed to first-timers who knew what they wanted but didn't really *know* what they *wanted*, made a few suggestions, all of which Amid found lacking: an encounter with a

Drauk, who existed only partially in this dimension, but whose visible appendages were second to none; an opportunity to participate in a Grue mating session (a race who notoriously required a group of five for the event); or perhaps a total submersion in a vat full of the gooey and very friendly Oolem?

Amid supposed he could see why these offers might be considered bizarre or exotic to someone who had never left their homeworld, but he himself required something more unusual still, and told the clerk so.

The clerk made several more suggestions, feeling out Amid's requirements. Sensory deprivation? Sensory *overload*? Humiliation? Mind-altering substances?

Amid brushed off every offer.

Unfazed, the clerk simply nodded, and said, "I think we have something for you. Come this way, please."

The clerk led Amid through a maze of corridors, all lined with secured doors. As they rounded a corner, the clerk said, "Behind this door is a machine. One standard session will cost you sixty-five thousand credits."

At last, something to raise Amid's eyebrows. Sixty-five was an exorbitant amount of money to spend at an establishment such as this – particularly when, as Amid was proud to say, he didn't really need to pay for it. However, the price, combined with the alluringly vague sell, was enough to get Amid's currency card out of his pocket and into the clerk's scanner.

"Thank you very much, sir." The clerk pressed his hand to the panel on the door, and it swung open. "Someone will come at the end of your session to escort you out."

The door swung shut, and latched again, as soon as Amid was inside. The room was dimly lit, but his eyes quickly adjusted so that he might see all of its features.

Or rather, it's feature: there was no bed, no chairs, no place to wash up. The only object in the room was the machine.

Flickering lights cast a soft glow on all sides of it, and its metallic surface gleamed warmly in the dim room. But as Amid walked all the way around it, examining every inch of it, he did not find any obvious way to interact with it sexually. Save for a few protrusions, it was essentially a cube, each side about the length of Amid's arm.

Amid knelt down to examine its features more closely. There were some buttons and switches, and he pressed and tugged at them until he found one that provoked a new hum from the machine, as well as the occasional beep. Many of the panel lights now glowed continuously, and a discreet display showed some characters in a Ku Pirrian dialect. He had, apparently, successfully turned it on.

However, it was still just a cube of indeterminate purpose. Amid ran his hands all along the surface, hoping to encounter a hidden panel or scanner which when touched would reveal a suitable orifice or protrusion that he might make use of. But he found nothing.

The clock was ticking on this session. He couldn't just flail about, hoping to bump into this machine's secret; he had to think. Resting his hands on the machine, Amid used his imagination to puzzle out precisely how he was going to get his 65,000 credits worth. As he did, the vibrations of the machine traveled through his hands and, after a while, down his arms, until he swore he could feel them in his guts. This gave him pause.

Perhaps he was losing his mind a little with frustration and impatience, but he could swear that the machine's little chirps were growing more inviting, as though it were softly pleading for him to find a way. The rumbling vibration was now making his spine tingle. Alright, Amid decided, enough with finding a way to properly have sex with this machine; he was going to get it in any way he possibly could.

Another survey of the cube brought to Amid's attention a lever that he had overlooked the first time. It was a long handle, protruding at about waist height (that is, waist-height where Amid was, still on his knees), with soft rubber at the end, contoured to match a Ku Pirrian's many-fingered grip. Amid placed two fingers against it, and the pulsating hum was even stronger. He shuffled forward and tilted his pelvis to press the handle against his half-hard cock through his trousers. It wasn't perfect, but the vibration sent a jolt through him, strangely satisfying after the struggle he'd been through.

As the friction brought him to full hardness, pre-come began to seep into the fabric of his trousers; Amid was loath to remove himself from the source of the vibration, but he did so just long enough to bring his cock out, which he held slightly at an angle, so that he could align it with the whole length of the lever. The soft rubber felt smoother on the tender skin of his cock than he anticipated, and he was able to rub it back and forth, feeling all the ridges and contours of the handle.

Leaning forward, he rested his chest and arms on the machine, clutching at it while he kept his cock carefully pressed to the lever, pushing hard to feel the vibrations as deeply as possible. When his cock began to slip a little, he reached down with one hand to hold it steady, so he could rut with abandon while never losing contact. As his pleasure spiraled higher, he began to grunt, humping the machine without shame or thought, until at last he let out a groan, and as he stilled, three powerful pulses of semen splashed against the side of the metal, spoiling its pristine surface.

Amid collapsed to the floor. He couldn't remember the last time he'd felt so satisfied, and he couldn't believe that this, of all things, had been what had done it for him. Perhaps it was the struggle, the challenge. Charming his way effortlessly from planet to planet, it had been a long time since he'd imagined that finding sexual satisfaction could ever be the least bit difficult. *That* was what he'd been missing.

Amid had an errand or two to run the following day, but when his duties were dispensed with, his mind wandered back to the discreet establishment in the entertainment district. That clerk had known exactly what he needed, practically on sight, and that level of customer service was hard to resist taking advantage of again. As night fell, Amid found himself back at that desk, in front of the same smoothly cordial clerk.

"I hope that you found your last visit to our establishment satisfactory?" the clerk said, a hint of a smile in his voice.

"I did," Amid said, "that's why I'm back. I was wondering if you had anything else going on that I might be interested in?"

The clerk browsed a screen on his desk for a moment, then said, "I think we have something for you. Do you like to watch?"

Voyeurism was not a particular inclination of Amid's, but after choosing the machine for him last time, Amid was willing to put a lot of trust in the clerk. "I like it okay. What will I be watching?"

"Follow me, please," the clerk said.

After another journey down a seemingly interminable series of corridors, there was a pause, where the clerk informed Amid that this session would cost him 8,000 credits. That was an unbelievable bargain, compared to what yesterday had cost him, and Amid gladly paid. The clerk then opened the door for him.

Behind this door were several other patrons, which did not concern Amid; he had no reputation to sully by being seen in this kind of place. And anyway, the other patrons were not looking at him. Their faces were pressed into viewing goggles. One empty set of goggles remained, and Amid assumed they were for him. He sat in the station and leaned down, aligning himself and pressing his face into the goggles.

Through the goggles, Amid watched a naked male humanoid – shaped similarly to himself, but not a native of his homeworld – darting madly around a small, sparsely-furnished room, attempting to interact with a shifting cluster of bright pink and very mobile blobs. At first Amid only saw three of these blobs, but as the man got close to leaping onto one of them, erection-first, the blob split into two more, leaving the man to belly-flop onto the mattress. The man did not seem at all discouraged; in fact, he was laughing. He continued to try to capture these jelly-like imps in his arms, or to tackle them bodily, and they continued to wiggle enticingly until the last possible instant, when they would evade him, bouncing around the room, teasing him. With each failed attempt, the man seemed more pleased. Through the earpieces, Amid could hear him talking to the blobs: "I'm gonna getcha!" he said with a grin, and launched himself again at his jiggly pink quarry.

Amid found this all very entertaining, though as it went on, he couldn't help but find himself wound tight with suspense: would the man catch one? What would happen when he did? Would he just stick his cock in it, or would they cling to all his limbs, and stimulate his whole body? Would they swallow him up? They looked delicious, though, in more ways than one; perhaps *he* swallow *them*? These were all interesting prospects, and Amid could not believe that he was, for the second time in as many days, feeling excitement that made him positively shake, after so long without so much as an inkling of a thrill.

"This is incredible," he said aloud, compelled to share his delight with someone, anyone else. "I've never seen anything like this before."

Next to him, a man chuckled. Neither of them lifted their faces from their goggles, but Amid's neighbor remarked, "You think *this* is great, you should have been here yesterday. A guy was in that room trying to figure out how to fuck a metal box."

SECRET MENU

ZINN WAS all settled down in his tiny windowless office and ready to dig in to the day's main project. It was not a glamorous job, transferring the organization's expansive and detailed fabrication criteria from the old system to the new, but Zinn was perfectly content with the dismally low level of excitement it offered – mainly because it came packaged with a comparable level of responsibility and stress. Today, like most other days, he'd prepared a hot drink, seated himself in front of his dual screens, queued an upbeat collection of music on his media player, adjusted the ergonomic settings of his chair to keep him from slumping, and was all ready to begin...

...when Blye tapped at his door, ducked his head inside, and said, "Time to go to the assembly."

Zinn tried to remain calm. "Can I skip it?"

"It's mandatory. If they catch you in here, you'll get a reprimand."

Zinn sighed, thinking of all the useless assemblies he'd had to attend in the past. Whatever this one was about, Zinn was certain that it could not be a better use of his time than being allowed to do his job. He shut off his media player and got up from his chair.

Zinn and Blye sat next to each other, as they usually did, with Flid and Vollo on either side of them. A snide comment here and there, a subtle nudge when the speaker said something that could be interpreted as humorous or naughty, these things had always helped the four of them endure the drudgery of these assemblies.

The Personnel Director made his way across the dais, and leaned into the microphone, softly saying, "Can everyone hear me?" Utter silence followed, as everyone assumed someone else around them would have the enthusiasm to confirm that the audio equipment was working. "Please join me in welcoming Plax, from the Delta Sector's Department of Civilian Hygiene."

A grinning fellow climbed the steps onto the dais while Zinn's assembled co-workers applauded half-heartedly. He confidently took the microphone from its stand, and began to pace back and forth across the stage with it, speaking into it with an insincerely casual tone.

"Thank so much for that, it's so good to be here, thank you for inviting me. I'm going to be talking to you today about something very important to you as Trevellians who value your safety, and value your well-being."

Plax paused a moment to fumble with the computer that sat on the podium, and soon, an image was projected on the giant screen behind him. It was a face, but not a face like Zinn's or Plax's. It was a tan face with hair around it and a protruding nose.

"Some of you may have seen these folks around lately. They're called humans. Some call them Earthlings, or you may have heard some other slang terms for them, like 'short-necks' or 'water-drinkers,' but we're going to call them humans, because that's their preferred term. That's what they call themselves."

Plax pressed a button on the computer, and next to this human face appeared the words: **PROTECT YOURSELF FROM HUMANS.**

A murmur rolled through the crowd, and Zinn was suddenly a little nervous. Were humans something he needed to protect himself from? No one had said anything like that on the news, where footage of humans arriving at Trevellian spaceports had been shown with no cautionary comment.

"A little food for thought, huh?" Plax said with a chuckle, indicating the alarmist words on the screen. "It's true that humans are our most valuable allies against the Dropol Empire, and the only way they can get to the Z Region to fight those nasty Drops is to have a waypoint from which to assemble and refuel. They may not seem like a big deal, but you need to know the facts: these humans are overfed, they are overpaid, they are oversexed – and they are *over here*."

The audience, half-asleep when Plax had taken the stage, was now riveted. They wanted to hear all about these humans – especially the oversexed part.

On the screen, a map came up, as well as a few charts and graphs. "We're hosting about half a million humans here in Delta Sector at any given time. Each day thousands get their orders and ship out to Z Region, and each day thousands more arrive. Humans have access to lots of arable land in their systems of residence, so they show up here with plenty of rations, durable fiber clothing, everything they need.

"But humans also like a good time, so while they're here, they want to spend their pay on drinks, entertainment, and on folks like you, who might be willing to show them that good time. And what could be the harm in that, right? If a human wants to take you someplace nice to eat, to watch a show, that sounds like your lucky day, right?"

There was a subdued assent from the crowd, before Plax shook his head and said, "Nuh-uh. Because humans don't just want your company and your conversation. Humans want to have sex with you."

This revelation made Zinn's heart skip a beat. Humans were strangers, absolute strangers, only here for a short time, and in that short time they wanted to have sex? There wasn't anything wrong with having sex, but only under a very specific set of circumstances, the first of which was, you and the other person had to know each other for ten or twenty years. It took at least ten years in each other's company before your minds fell into harmony, before you could become close enough to complete the physical act without the discordant notes of the other's mind driving you mad.

Everyone else in the crowd seemed equally mystified by the idea of having sex with a strange human, how it would even be possible. So Plax explained:

"Humans have no real empathy. Even if you are standing next to them, they can only tell what's going on in your mind if you speak your thoughts and intentions or act them out physically. Their underdeveloped brains feel no discord during the sexual act, nor do they emanate any. But in no way should we treat their cold, unfeeling minds as advantageous. Not only is there no discord, there is no harmony. There is only the physical act itself, and the pleasures that result are only the meaningless physical ones. And humans don't care! They will mate with you, they will form a primitive, parasitical attachment to you, and after that, you will be unable to bond properly with one of your own kind."

This revelation was particularly shocking to the crowd. Having sex with a human could ruin you for other Trevellians? This was a grave consequence.

"Now, let's take a closer look at humans, what they look like, and what characteristics they possess." Plax clicked to the next slide, and a variety of humans, all of them unclothed, appeared on the screen. "Humans, as you can see here, come in many different colors."

Someone in the audience raised their hand. "Why?"

Plax hesitated. "You know, we don't have a lot of information on that, but we suspect it functions as a form of camouflage on their homeworld. Anyway. So you see these thick legs? Humans have powerfully muscled legs, because they are stalking predators. Their bodies were built for it, and so their minds became adapted to it. I know some of you are out there saying, 'But I met a human once, and they didn't attempt to interact with me sexually.' Perhaps it didn't appear that way, but that's because humans are in it for the long game. A human might hang around their intended target, *you*, for months, before taking their opportunity.

"It may not seem likely to you, that humans would want to mate with you. After all, *they* don't look good to *us*, right?" This got a fairly ambiguous collective response from the audience. Plax prompted: "No, they don't. But humans aren't like us; they are attracted indiscriminately to any kind of life form that might let them near. I've read some human literature, folks, and let me tell you, humans love to get attached to a person of another species, and they will cling to that person, even if it means that person must stay stranded on Earth forever, even if it means they must give up their unique abilities. Humans don't care about anything but their own sexual desires."

Plax kept dropping meaningful pauses into his lecture, during which time Zinn wondered, *Is this a cue that we are supposed to be thinking deeply about what he's just said?* He felt similar confusion from those nearest to him. And apparently Plax did intend this, for he continued:

"I'm sure all of you out there are thinking the same thing: 'Oh, that'll never happen to me. I won't fall victim to a human's wiles. I'm smarter than that. How could a human even have sex with me? This isn't compatible.'" Plax gestured to the area between the human's legs. "Let me tell you something: humans are insatiable, and they are not particularly concerned with what your genitals look like. They have been known to engage in sexual congress with any kind of orifice, any kind of digit. They have attempted it with flaps, with bony ridges, with cartilaginous protrusions. They are not picky. And who wants to be with someone who's not picky? Not us, right? We respect ourselves, right?" Again, the crowd agreed with this statement, but not with an incredible amount of enthusiasm.

"So what are the primary stalking grounds of humans?" As Plax spoke, each location that he listed popped up on the screen. "*Spaceports*, the most obvious location. And an excellent reminder that humans are here for a good time, not a long time. But while they're here, humans also tend to congregate wherever there are *restaurants* and *nightclubs*, and the lower the reputation of those establishments, the more likely you'll find them there. You can also find them in the *souvenir shops*, no doubt buying cheap tokens to send to the string of mating partners they've left behind on other worlds.

"Alright, now that I've made it clear why humans are dangerous, and where you should exercise particular caution, I'm going to leave you with some helpful phrases, things you can say if a human approaches you. Practice saying these things, especially if you plan to visit one of the places where you're likely to encounter a human."

The phrases appeared one by one on the screen. Plax read out the first one: "*No, thank you.* Say it with me." The audience repeated the phrase, in unison. "Humans think it's polite to thank someone even if you are refusing what they're offering. With any luck, a human will accept your polite refusal and walk away.

"*I'm married.* 'Married' is a word you'll have to memorize phonetically. Because they are so emotionally stunted, when humans choose a long-term partner, they tend to want to make the union legally binding, in order for it to seem real and legitimate. If you tell a human you are 'married' to someone, they will think of you as being the property of your partner, and should at that point stop thinking of you as a potential target.

"Finally, if all else fails: *I have a disease.* Humans are intelligent enough to fear diseases and to understand how they are transmitted. If all else fails, suggesting a risk of disease is usually enough to discourage them from trying to mate with you.

"To conclude: do not let the novelty of a human presence on Trevell blind you. Respect yourselves, and stick to suitable life mates. Thank you for your time, and be safe out there, everyone!"

After a round of brief, polite applause, Zinn and his co-workers stood up and began to make their way back to work, at varying speeds, depending on how much pressure they were under to deliver a project on time. Zinn nudged his way past several people, in more of a hurry than most. But Blye, Flid, and Vollo were close behind him, and when they got out into the courtyard, and the crowd began to dissipate, Zinn was inundated with their chatter:

"Humans sound really exciting!" Vollo said. "I barely knew that humans were even here, but after everything Plax said, now I really want to have sex with one!"

"Me too!" Flid said. "I'm going to go to the city center tonight and see if I can find one! Plax said it felt good to have sex with a human, and I want to find out!"

"I'll come with you," Blye said. Zinn's friends had always been like this, obsessed with sex, and eager for the opportunity to have it. Not yet having met other Trevellians with whom they had achieved harmony, their opportunities were severely limited, but they loved to talk about it.

"What about you?" Vollo asked Zinn. "You want to come with?"

"I can't, I'm busy," Zinn said, a lie that he elaborated on by saying, "I'm helping my cousin, uh, move."

"Your loss," said Vollo.

"This is going to be so great!" said Flid. "I'm going to find a human to have sex with my flaps! What about you?"

Blye said, "I'm going to find a human to have sex with my ridges!"

"Ooh, that's a good idea too!"

Zinn was quiet. He just wanted to get back to work, and to forget all about the very weird assembly.

Zinn hadn't intended to pick up twelve books at the library. It had just sort of...happened. Having read every book about Trevell's Great Remaking that he could load onto his holoreader, then having checked out every old-fashioned paper book at the library nearest his home, Zinn had made his way across town to the Central Library, in search of more books about the Great Remaking that had not yet been converted to a digital format. He'd only found two, but he hadn't seen any harm in just browsing a little...and had ended up with ten more books, mostly novels about heroes whose adventures were set in the Remaking period. It was only when the stack of books he carried was tucked up under his chin that he accepted that it was time to go to the check-out station.

On his way out of the stacks, he was met by another patron, wearing a strange uniform, who asked, "Excuse me, do you work here?"

Zinn looked the person up and down. The skin tone, the hair, the eyes, it all matched the slide from Plax's cautionary seminar.

Zinn gasped, "You're a human!"

"I sure am," the human said with a polite smile.

Zinn looked down the aisles to see if anyone was nearby. But they were alone. Zinn whispered, "Are you going to try to have sex with me?"

The human cocked his head as he laughed. "Um...no."

Zinn's shoulders slumped. "Oh."

"I just needed someone to help me with this cartridge. I don't know how to use the machines." The human held up a silver cartridge, the kind that old movies were archived on.

"I don't work here, but I can show you how to use those," Zinn said. "Come this way."

Zinn took the human to a bank of viewing machines. He set his books down on a table, then turned to take the cartridge from the human, but when he did so, he watched the human's jaw drop. Zinn followed the human's gaze, looking down at what he was gawping at.

"Is that a League of Intrepid Adventurers symbol?"

"Oh, that." Zinn touched the pendant of the necklace he wore. The human was entirely correct. Zinn loved all the League of Intrepid Adventurers books, even though most Trevellians thought of them as being for children. He wore the necklace in case he might get to have a conversation with another fan who saw him wearing it in public. But this was not someone with whom he'd expected that to happen. "I never would have guessed that someone from another planet would know about the League," he said, excited but bashful.

"We just got the first three books on Earth," the human said. "But I know there are like, a hundred."

"A hundred and seven," Zinn gently corrected. "Yes, the League has been around for eighty-three years. I guess it takes a while for things to get from here to Earth."

"That's why I was excited to come to Trevell. Before I ship out to the Z Region, I want to read all the League stuff I can – and see the movies. That's what this cartridge is, actually: the first League movie."

Zinn couldn't help but smile; the first League film was...not great. But he had first seen it when he was very young, too young to think of it as anything but magical. "You shouldn't watch that movie here, in a library. These screens are so small, and I don't know if our headsets would fit you."

"I know, but beggars can't be choosers. I've got to see it however I can, while I've got the chance."

"I have a copy at my home," Zinn blurted out, before he could think better of it. But having said it, he couldn't help but go on. "And a much bigger screen. And I haven't watched it in a while."

"Are you inviting me over?"

"I guess I am," Zinn said, cringing at his own foolishness. Hadn't he just learned the other day that humans were the most dangerous perverts in the galaxy? And now he was disregarding his own personal safety, just because he'd met one who was a fan of the League?

But this couldn't be one of *those* humans. He was so polite, and he looked so sweet, with his sticky-outy ears and his funny clothes. And he must not have seen Zinn cringe just then, because he eagerly took Zinn up on his offer. "Do you live near here? Are you busy tonight?"

Zinn looked at his stack of historical novels. He couldn't exactly claim that he had a busy social life, could he? "I'm free tonight. Let me check these out, and we can take the Pneumatic back to my home."

"Sounds good. I'm Beau, by the way." The human stuck out his hand.

"Oh, I'm Zinn." Zinn mirrored Beau's gesture, and with some additional guidance from Beau, they shook hands.

Zinn's mind was racing as he and Beau made their way to the check-out station. He had to think of a way to make this happen without being a complete idiot about it. When Beau excused himself to return the movie cartridge, Zinn too out his pocket messenger sent a quick note to Blye, saying that he was taking someone home, and to please check in with him a couple hours from then, to make sure he was okay.

Blye messaged back: *You little tart. Go get 'em!*

But Zinn didn't see that message. The whole way home, he was preoccupied with the conversation he was having with Beau. It began on the walk to the Pneumatic: Zinn asked, "So, who's your favorite League member?"

"Oh, I like them all," Beau said, "but if I had to choose, I think it would be Zorb. He's hilarious. What about you?"

"My favorite? Is Melbo." Zinn was met with a blank stare. "Wait, you haven't seen Melbo yet, he doesn't appear until the fourth book. Well, Melbo was built by – oh dear, I really shouldn't tell you anything, it would ruin the surprise! Okay, well, my favorite *original* League member, I think, would be Wrok..."

They did not stop talking until they reached Zinn's door. The whole trip took an hour, but to Zinn it seemed like only minutes, it had been so enthralling. As he invited Beau inside, he apologized for it not being very tidy. "I didn't know I would have a guest."

"It's okay, really, I'm just so excited to see the movie."

Zinn scanned through his movie collection until he found *Dawn of the League of Intrepid Adventurers*. "Don't get your hopes up too high. It's less than perfect, and the actor who plays Zorb is...they got a different actor to play him in all the later movies. But this will be fun! When I was young, I watched this over and over. I'll try not to recite the whole thing."

Plax had been right about human minds – they did not broadcast anything. Try as he might, Zinn felt no harmony, no discord, nothing from Beau. But while this was frustrating at times, not being able to receive the simplest things, such as if Beau was enjoying himself, the challenge of reading Beau's body language was a fun puzzle.

And Beau wasn't really that perplexing when it came to physical expression. He watched the movie raptly – every once in a while, Zinn would peek over at him, and never did he see Beau giggle at the over-the-top acting or the sub-par visual effects. He was entranced, devouring every frame of what had been known for decades as the kind of movie you would watch with your friends and make fun of. It warmed Zinn's heart. And the whole time, Beau did not try to sit closer to Zinn, or otherwise interrupt the movie with any of the predatory behavior that, according to Plax, humans indulged in compulsively.

Afterward, Beau exclaimed, "That was so cool!"

Zinn looked at the clock. "We could watch the next one."

"Oh, I can't, I'm sorry," Beau said, his smile disappearing for a moment. "I have to be at evening roll call in an hour. But when are you free? I do want to watch the second one."

They set the soonest possible date to see each other again, and in the meantime, Zinn gave Beau a paper copy of the fourth League book. "If you bring a holoreader with you next time, I can copy the whole collection to you."

"I will. Hey, next time, would you like to have dinner first? Anywhere you like." Beau gestured to the book in his hand. "It's my treat for you being so generous."

"Then let's meet at The Number Forty-Two. I've never been there, but I've walked by it a lot. It's a human-owned restaurant. They serve human food there."

Beau's eyes lit up. "That would be wonderful! I miss home cooking. All I get here is rations."

"You'll have to tell me what to order there, though. I've never had human food." Another glance at the clock told Zinn he was being rude. "I'm sorry, I won't keep you any longer. Go to your roll call so you don't get in trouble!"

Beau waved as he walked away, and Zinn waved back, though he didn't know why; it just seemed right to return his guest's gesture.

Just then, he got a message from Blye:

Everything going okay? I want to hear ALL about it at lunch tomorrow.

Zinn messaged back: *Nothing happened. We just watched Dawn of the League.*

Blye did not reply right away. In fact, Zinn had time to perform his entire evening grooming ritual and get into bed before he got a message back:

Nerds.

The next day, after work, Zinn ignored all the books he'd checked out from the library, and instead re-read the first League book, his lifelong but occasionally dormant obsession with the franchise rekindled once again. A prime factor in his reading choice was Beau – Zinn found it difficult to concentrate on anything at all, distracted as he was by thoughts of Beau, but a League book was the most appealing way he could come up with to pass the time until Zinn could see him again – a book that they both loved.

Walking to The Forty-Two on the day they had agreed upon, Zinn felt like he was floating six inches off the ground, he was so excited to see Beau again. And when he arrived, he saw the most wonderful thing: Beau's big, bright smile at the sight of *him*.

Beau held the door open for Zinn to pass through. "So is there a reason it's called 'Forty-Two'?" Zinn asked.

"I suppose it's because forty-two is kind of a sacred number in some places on Earth. It has this, like, deep significance." Beau admitted he didn't know much more about it than that, and was shortly thereafter distracted by the prospect of eating human food. "This is gonna be so great. You're gonna love–" Beau stopped halfway between the door and the counter, and sniffed the air. "Huh," he said.

Above the counter there hung a menu with full-color illustrations. Zinn looked to Beau to make recommendations, but Beau just stood there, grimacing, his eyes increasingly despondent. Zinn read some of the menu items aloud:

"Luht-ee-fisk...am I pronouncing that correctly?"

Beau just stared at the menu and said, "I don't believe this."

"Kim chee-*ee*? For how long do you say the 'e' part?"

Beau walked up to the counter, where another human greeted him with enthusiasm: "How you doin'? What can I get you?"

"Hey, man," Beau said. "do you have any curry, or ramen, or burgers or something?"

The cashier leaned forward and said, "Don't worry, buddy, we got a secret menu for humans." He gestured to the sign above him. "This is just what the locals are into. You cannot pickle enough foods for these guys. We've been pickling things you can't imagine." He glanced at Zinn. "No offense, hey. What can I get you, though?"

Beau said, "You got like a sampler platter of the good stuff? My friend has never had Earth food before."

"No problem." The cashier hollered to the kitchen, "A number Forty-Two!" The kitchen staff hollered back, lifting their hands to greet a fellow human.

"I was wondering why I didn't see any other humans when we came in," Beau remarked. And indeed, while they waited for their meal, Zinn looked around, and all he saw were fellow Trevellians, digging into natto, vieux-bologne, surströmming, and chòu dòufu.

Beau explained that while all of those dishes were authentic foods from Earth, they were "specialty dishes," enjoyed by people with "specific palettes." He hesitated before choosing these phrases, prompting Zinn to ask, "Are you being diplomatic?"

"Yes," Beau sighed. "Yes, I am. But hey, if your people love that food, that's fine, I mean, maybe I was rude not to let you order..."

"No," said Zinn, "I want to eat what you like."

On the table were plastic mats with a flattened-out map of the Earth on them, and Beau pointed out where all the really good foods came from: pasta, phở, chicken tikka, pad thai, pizza, french fries.

"Where are you from?" Zinn asked.

"I was born here," Beau said, pointing. "But my ancestors are from all over this map. See, where I was born, it's a rich country, everyone's well-fed and safe. But some of my ancestors are from here." He pointed to the other side of the map. "There was a terrible war, so they fled. And others lived over here, for thousands of years, but the sea levels rose and their whole island disappeared, so they had to leave. And then some of my folks were from here, but there was a famine. So they all showed up at different times to the rich country, and they all met each other, and had babies, and those babies had babies, and then there was me."

The whole story was so grim, but this last part in particular made Zinn blanch. "The babies had babies?"

"No, no! The babies grew up, and then they had babies." Beau laughed. "I guess they don't teach you guys anything about humans here, huh?"

Zinn thought about how to answer this question for a split second before deciding the correct response, for the time being, was "Nothing at all."

Beau explained how long humans lived, and how many children they tended to have, and how long it took them to grow up. It sounded to Zinn like Beau was about a quarter of the way into his life cycle. Zinn asked more questions, and Beau answered them, at least until the meal arrived, at which point he explained what all the foods were, and why they were delicious.

Zinn tried them all, and while nothing tasted offensive, he found everything bland, despite Beau's insistence that this or the other thing was "salty" or "spicy." Zinn looked with some longing at the other tables, whose meals he could smell from where he was; they were delightfully pungent. But it didn't matter too much. He was happy just to be in Beau's company.

Beau spun a description of one of the foods in the sampler into a story of a comical adventure involving himself and his two siblings – a small mess in the kitchen, once they attempted to hide it from their parents, became a colossal mess, injuring no one but providing "epic" punishments and familial running jokes for years afterward. As Beau finished the story, though, he caught himself. "I'm sorry, I've been so rude, talking about myself this whole time."

"No, it's fine," Zinn said, trying not to sound too enamored. "It's fine. I think you're really interesting."

"I want to know about you, though. Here I am staying on your planet, watching movies in your home, and I've hardly gotten to know you. Tell me about you."

"There's not much to tell," Zinn said, looking down at his half-eaten food.

"Well, have you got someone special in your life?"

"Oh, like a mate? No, I'm just so busy with my work, and you know, I've got my books..."

If he were honest, neither of these things prevented Zinn from being involved with someone. But he hoped Beau would believe him, because it was better than the truth: that he was just shy and boring.

Zinn started to explain what his job was, then went on to how he'd been selected for that job, then about the schools he'd been to, and then his favorite subject in school: the Great Remaking. Beau asked what the Great Remaking was, and Zinn launched into an elaborate explanation, delighted to not have to talk about himself anymore. Beau seemed to understand what the Great Remaking was about, and told Zinn that Earth had also experienced several societal collapses that had been followed by a long period of stagnation and then at last a flourishing of art, philosophy, and science.

"My favorite League story is the one where they go back in time to the Great Remaking," Zinn said. "That's what got me interested in studying the actual history of it."

"Oh, we were going to watch another League movie tonight, weren't we?" Beau looked at the clock on the wall. "I totally forgot, I've just been enjoying this conversation so much. There's still time, though, if we left now."

Beau agreed with Zinn's assertion, that the second League movie was far superior to the first, less corny and more true to the spirit of the books, and that the new actor playing Zorb was much better. "And Rrodar was a great villain," Beau said, "he was evil, but he was a little fun, too. Villains in stories like these should be a little fun."

"Yes, absolutely! The first movie barely even had a villain, it was trying to be so philosophical. Like, the villain was just an idea that pervades society, and that's no fun at all. I can read books about that. Oh, that reminds me: did you bring your holoreader?"

Beau took his reader from jacket and handed it over, and by holding his own close to it, Zinn was able to transfer data to Beau's. "There," he said, "now you have all the League books, plus there's an anthology of newsletters from the Society Of League Enthusiasts, and a couple of other books, *The Real Science Behind the League* and so on. You don't have to read all that, it's just in case."

"No, I will! Listen." Beau put his hand on Zinn's shoulder. Zinn did not think it possible to both jump out of his skin and melt at the same time, but he felt ready to do both, just at the touch of Beau's hand. "I don't want to go, but I really have to. But at the end of the week, I have one night with no curfew. I have to report early in the morning, but I can stay late, and we'll have enough time to watch two movies, even!"

"That would be amazing," Zinn said. He put his hand over the one on his shoulder, and continued to hold it even as he walked Beau to the door. "I had a really good time. Thank you for buying me real Earth food and watching the movie with me and all that."

"It was my pleasure." Beau clung to Zinn's hand, even as he stepped out into the corridor. "Goodbye," he said slowly, walking backwards as he left, so he could continue smiling at Zinn until he disappeared around the corner.

The moment Zinn shut the door, he began to shake with the joy of what had just happened. When the thing he was feeling got to be too much, Zinn released a trill of excitement, his arms wrapped around himself in rapture.

For the next two days, while he waited for the end of the week to arrive, all Zinn could think about was Beau. Every song he listened to reminded him of Beau. Flicking through a magazine on his lunch break, Zinn lingered on the fashion advertisements, which he'd never done before, imagining Beau wearing those clothes. How handsome he would look in them! Not like that silly uniform he was always in. It was clean and fit him well, but it was silly. Beau would have to see a tailor, to have his Trevellian clothes customized, as he was a little differently proportioned, but once it was done he would look so nice.

Ordering groceries, Zinn went overboard with snacks and drinks, choosing lots of things that Beau might like, if he were interested in traditional Trevellian food during his next visit.

And of course, every time he thought about something to do with the League, which was often, he reflexively wondered what Beau would think of this or that book or movie, when he got to it.

In those two days of waiting, Zinn also thought of lots of things he could talk about with Beau – even some things about himself. He was better prepared now, to come up with something interesting if Beau asked him to talk about himself again.

But when he answered the door, and saw Beau standing there, he forgot everything except how much he'd missed Beau's smile. He managed to invite Beau in, but was too excited about being in Beau's presence to say much, although he reasoned that was a good thing, lest he start babbling incessantly. Beau wandered over to a huge tray of snacks on the kitchen table. "Ooh, are these for us? I'm starving."

"Yes! I didn't know what you might like, so I made a lot of different things." That wasn't quite the truth; Zinn had gotten some idea about the foods Beau liked from the sampler at the restaurant, and had prepared the blandest, starchiest foods, the ones that were staples in the temperate but culturally remote places on Trevell.

To Zinn's delight, Beau loved them, trying a little bit of everything but devouring all the tuber puffs and root crisps while they watched *League of Intrepid Adventurers: In Time*.

Zinn spent a lot of the movie looking surreptitiously at Beau, watching him put the morsels of food in his mouth and savor them. He couldn't believe it, because they barely knew each other, but Zinn was having an overwhelming feeling like he might want to take off his clothes, or have Beau take off his clothes, and...but no. That was the sort of thing Blye, Flid, and Vollo might do, but not him. Zinn did do something very bold, though, in his opinion: halfway through the movie, he got up to get something else to drink, and when he sat down, he sat much closer to Beau, close enough that their legs touched. And Beau didn't even seem to mind. Then Zinn couldn't concentrate on watching the movie – that is, until the climactic scene, which made Beau gasp and clutch Zinn's knee. Only then did Zinn remember – he'd seen this movie so many times, he'd forgotten how sad the ending was, especially if one didn't know how things would be resolved in the next movie.

"But Fieron can't die," was all Beau could say when the movie was over. "Is Fieron really dead? Does he come back? They must know a way to bring him back."

"I can't just *tell* you," Zinn demurred. "You have to watch the next one and find out."

"Let's watch it right now!"

"Oh, but that's no fair. I had to wait two years to find out if Fieron was really dead. You shouldn't get to find out in two minutes. I'll tell you what: let's just wait until the next time you come over. That'll only be a few days, right?"

Beau looked down. "Well, no, actually. This is my last day on Trevell. My division is shipping out for the Z Region tomorrow."

Zinn's mouth fell open. He felt like his guts had suddenly vaporized, like he was empty inside. "Why didn't you tell me that before?"

"I didn't want you to be thinking about it. *I* didn't want to think about it." Beau took both Zinn's hands in his own. "I just wanted to enjoy the time I got to spend with you."

Zinn's throat was tight, but he managed to croak, "So this is the last time I'll ever see you?"

"Only until I get back from the war."

"But what if you don't come back?"

Beau made a dismissive noise. "I wouldn't worry about that. I fly fighter drones. Guys like me are in a lot less danger than the infantry. I'm not going to see any real action. And then I'll be back here before you know it."

Of course Beau would have a nice job, like flying drones; he was very smart. And Zinn wanted to believe that Beau was telling the truth, and not lying to make him feel better. He squeezed both Beau's hands, looking at them so he wouldn't have to look into Beau's eyes when he said what he was about to say. "Beau, you're so brave, going to fight in that war. I want to do something special for you before you go." Zinn turned his face away. "But I don't know if it's something you want from me. I don't want to be presumptuous."

Beau gently touched Zinn's cheek, encouraging Zinn to turn and face him again. "I think I know what you're talking about, and I would like it very much. But not if it's because you feel sorry that I'm leaving; only if it's because you genuinely like me."

Zinn insisted, "I do! You're amazing! But you should probably know, I haven't done it with–" He almost said *anyone*, but instead he said "...with a human before, so you'll have to show me how."

"I'm sure we can figure out how to have a good time. Do you have a bedroom...?"

Zinn stood up, still gripping Beau's hands, and led him there.

The light from the living room gave the bedroom a little warm illumination, so Zinn left it at that and didn't turn the light on. For a moment, the two of them just stood there, eager but too polite to pounce, until they both fell into giggles.

"Do you want to take my clothes off first?" Beau asked. "Then you can see what humans have got going on, and decide if you want to continue."

"There are at least two reasons why I want to get those silly clothes off you," Zinn said, and then laughed some more.

Beau helped with a couple of the fasteners, but other than that let Zinn go at his own pace, revealing his body inch by inch, limb by limb. Once his jacket and shirt were on the floor, Beau laid down on the bed, and Zinn climbed on top of him, exploring him. Beau's arms were thick with muscle, and when he flexed them, the muscles bulged even more. Zinn carefully felt all around them, poking the firm flesh, stroking the smooth skin. He petted the hair on Beau's chest, raked his fingers through it – and followed it down, to where it tapered into a line that disappeared beneath his trousers. Zinn wanted to see the rest of it, so he unbuttoned Beau's trousers and leaned over to yank them off, and to his surprise, a stiff cock sprang out and nearly smacked him in the face.

"Oh, haha, hello!" Zinn said, laughing. Then he paused, to stare not at Beau's erection, but what hung beneath it.

"Are these your...do you keep yours on the outside?" Curiosity overcame any embarrassment Zinn might have felt, and he rolled Beau's balls in his hand, fascinated.

"That's the standard issue, I'm afraid," Beau said.

"Oh, it's fine! It's just a surprise. But this is all fine. Your penis is almost the same as mine."

Beau's eyebrows went up. "*Almost* like yours? What's different about it?"

"Here, look." Zinn jumped off the bed and wiggled out of his clothes. Beau propped himself up on his elbows to get a better look, as Zinn showed him: his own cock was indeed similarly sized and shaped – except for the even, parallel ridges running all the way down Zinn's shaft. Beau gazed in awe, then reached out to feel each of these ridges, fleshy but firm; they caught on his encircling thumb and first finger as he slid it up and down.

"I hope it's alright," Zinn said, "and not too weird?"

"No, listen, that is..." Beau trailed off for a moment, seemingly mesmerized. "That is very nice. I like it, and I think I might like it even more by the end of the evening."

"I like yours, too!" Zinn climbed back onto the bed, and onto Beau. "What do you like to do with it? Where do humans put it?"

Beau laughed. "To start with, we can put it in your mouth, if you're interested in trying that."

"Like this?" With one elbow propping himself and the other hand on Beau's thigh, Zinn gave Beau's shaft the lightest brush of a kiss. Then he raised his head and said, "Like that?"

"Just like that," Beau sighed.

Zinn held Beau's sleek, unridged cock steady with his hand and administered firm kisses up and down the length of it. His tongue emerged from between his slightly parted lips, and touched the place where Beau's foreskin was stretched around the moist, flushed head. Just before engulfing it with his mouth, he said, "I love the way it smells and tastes."

Beau sighed, "Why am I not surprised by that."

Zinn had no idea whether he was doing it right, but Beau wasn't correcting him, so he kept going, suckling at the head, licking up all the sharply salty fluid that emerged from the tip. He was enjoying himself immensely, and judging by the noises Beau made, he seemed to be enjoying it as well. But then he gently nudged Zinn away.

"Oh," Zinn said, wiping the drool from his lower lip, "was I not doing it well?"

"You were doing it *too* well. I don't want to finish yet. I want you to put yours inside me first."

"In your mouth?"

Beau smiled. "No."

"Well, then...*oh*." Zinn looked between Beau's legs, then grabbed his thighs and shoved them apart, to see if he understood what Beau was implying. He did. "Humans have one too!" he said. "But if we're going to do that, you should put yours in me. I've never done it before, and I don't want to hurt you."

"You won't hurt me, if you follow my instruction. It just takes a little patience. And I'd really like to have yours in me. But have you got anything to ease the way? We can't do without it."

Zinn blinked. "Anything like what?"

"Like oil, maybe?"

"Oh, something slippery! Yes!"

Zinn darted out into the kitchen, returning with a bottle of oil. "I cook with this, I hope that's not weird."

Beau opened the bottle and sniffed the contents.

Zinn said, "So I just put this on my, um..."

"Not quite yet. First you should use your fingers to get me ready. I'm going to lie here on my back, and I'll keep an eye on you, alright?"

Beau took Zinn's hand and guided it to where Zinn had been looking, a minute ago. "Just put your fingers down here. You'll feel it."

With two slick fingers extended, Zinn pushed down into the warm crease. "Oh." It was one thing to see it, but he shivered at the sudden realization that he was touching it; that place was very private and special. "I can't believe you're letting me do this to you."

"You haven't even done it yet." Beau took Zinn's hand again. "Just push. *Gently*."

Zinn pressed against the little dip he felt with the pad of his finger. The hard muscle slammed shut at his touch, despite Beau's professed desire. "Sorry. I'm trying not to," Beau said. "It's just...it's been a while." He laid flat on his back and stared at the ceiling. "Okay, you push, I push."

Zinn tried again, and this time his finger breached and slid right in. He fought against the resisting muscle as it quivered. "It's so tight." Zinn whispered, urgently concerned. Beau continued to talk him through it, helped him get a second finger inside, and demonstrated how and where to crook them to touch just the right place inside him.

"You – *oh* – you feel that little bump right there?"

"Yes."

"Now, you don't have to stab at it. A little goes a long way. But keep rubbing that."

Zinn gently massaged the bump, watching Beau's face for feedback. "Like this?"

"Oh God, yeah."

Beau was sort of...wriggling, now. Watching him made Zinn want to wriggle, as well. He kept on doing just as Beau had told him. And despite the long minutes that went by, the novelty of the pleasure did not seem to ebb. Beau's cock, untouched, bobbed and twitched, and a thick, continuous strand of pre-ejaculate oozed out and touched his belly. Zinn could see it coming out, and watched carefully. The noises Beau uttered made it difficult to concentrate, though. Zinn said, "How will I know when you're ready for intercourse?"

Beau laughed at this inquiry. "I'm ready now. I'm, uh, really ready." He spread his thighs wide, tense and trembling. Between them, his balls were tight against his body, not hanging like they had been before. Zinn examined Beau's cock: What had been a barely visible slit at the tip was now pouting slightly open, and fluid was still coming readily. It was all very interesting.

Zinn hesitated. "How do we arrange ourselves?"

"That's up to you," said Beau.

"But I don't know what the optimal arrangement is."

"There's no one optimal arrangement. Just close your eyes and think: What do you want it to be like? Do you want to lie back while I ride you? Do you want to be able to look into my eyes? Do you want to just grab at me and pound away?"

After some thought, Zinn said, "I want...as much of you as possible to be touching as much of me as possible."

"Then we should spoon." Beau poured a palmful of oil from the bottle and spread it on Zinn's cock with a slow, tight stroke, which made Zinn shiver and which he stopped doing far too soon, in Zinn's opinion. Then he turned onto his side, away from Zinn, and said, "Just come up behind me, here."

Now even more eager for contact, Zinn pressed himself up against Beau's back, his slickened cock sliding into the cleft of Beau's behind. Beau was right; they could touch from head to toe this way. One of his arms was sort of trapped, but with the other Zinn could continue to explore Beau's body, and anything he couldn't reach with his arm, he could nuzzle with his chin or prod with his toes.

Beau said, "I may make noise where it'll be difficult to tell if you're causing pain or pleasure. If you don't hear me say 'stop,' then just keep doing whatever you're doing."

With his free hand, Zinn held his cock just behind the head. He slid it up and down blindly until he found where he was supposed to be going. Then he looked down at himself, where he was all set to join with Beau's body. "Do I just push it in?"

"Yes, just push it in."

"How far do I push it in before I should pull it out again?"

"Just do what comes naturally."

"This doesn't come naturally, that's the problem!"

"Zinn, please relax. When you get in there, you'll know what to do."

So Zinn pushed. And once again Beau was right; it was slow going but it was smooth. He pushed some more, a few nervous, incomplete strokes, feeling out the tantalizing resistance.

Beau arched toward him, groaning, "That's so good, those ridges feel *sooo* good." He continued to push back, taking an inch at a time, well after Zinn had stilled. Though frozen in shock, Zinn had an iron grip on Beau's hip, and that perhaps hindered Beau's ability to move, because he suggested, "It, ah, it feels better if you move a bit, as well."

"I'm sorry, I'm sorry." Zinn came back to himself and began to thrust again. Now Beau held still, and let Zinn give it to him. Zinn was perfectly silent, leaving plenty of space for Beau's coos and grunts of pleasure to fill the room.

Zinn's continued to push, working hard to do what Beau wanted, and he gasped, "What does it feel like? To have me inside you?"

"It feels like..." Beau hesitated for a moment, then blurted, "It feels like we're making love. Oh, I can't believe I just said that. But it's like my most secret guilty pleasure. When everything's quiet and slow, and you're just wrapping your arms and legs around each other and whispering to each other. I know it's not the sort of thing a guy is supposed to – *oh* – say, but I think making love is more intense than fucking."

Zinn kept his pace, but the whole experience suddenly became quite different for him. Beau was being very candid, but not in the crass, silly way that his friends were sometimes candid. And he was being so emotional, even though at the assembly Plax had said that humans didn't have feelings. Beau clearly did, even if he seemed embarrassed by them; he quickly moved the focus off himself by asking, "What does it feel like for you?"

"Oh, um." Zinn thought on it a moment. "I like touching your insides. I can't imagine anything more intimate."

Then they were quiet for a while, or rather, Zinn was quiet, continuing to thrust and listening to Beau's soft grunts. Finally, he said, "What were my other options before, for how we can do it?"

"Your what? Oh! You could lie on your back and I could ride you. Or you could pound away at me –"

"That! I want to do that. It sounds fun."

With some reluctance, Beau pulled himself away, allowing Zinn to slip out of him. They both uttered little bereft noises, and were eager to get close again. Beau rolled onto his elbows and knees, tilting his head to indicate that Zinn should get behind him with all haste. When Zinn's stiff, glistening cock passed by his line of sight, Beau muttered, “Yeah,” half to himself. “Put that magnificent thing back inside me.”

It already felt very different, just getting behind Beau. More like they were animals. Zinn took hold of Beau’s hip with one hand and aimed himself with the other.

“Don’t start going at it right away,” Beau said. “It’s going to be a bit different from this angle. Get a feel for it first.” Zinn did exactly what Beau told him to do, wishing to establish and maintain whatever cadence or effort was demanded of him. “That’s it. Nice and slow. Get me good and wanting it.”

Zinn liked hearing what Beau had to say. He wanted more of it. He asked, “Do you like doing it this way?”

Beau made a rumbling sound, deep in his throat, before admitting, “Yes. It feels so amazing, I don’t know why. I’ll take it any way, but nothing gets me going the way this does, just getting worked when I’m on my hands and knees. Yeah, that’s hitting it now.” As Zinn recovered his bearings and resumed his steady thrusting, Beau grunted, “Ah, *unh*, yeah.”

Zinn looked down, slack-jawed, watching himself pumping in and out of Beau’s hole, seeing how it took in, or gave up, each ridge of his shaft. It was so smooth and slick, he could just pump away, and hear and see how much Beau loved it. Beau’s whole body was shaking as he begged, “Faster. Faster. Harder.”

Zinn felt a twinge at hearing him so enraptured, and he suddenly wanted to hold Beau in his arms and see his beautiful smile. But in this position, he couldn’t. “Can we change again?” he asked. “Can we face each other?”

It took Beau longer to answer this time, but he finally rasped, “Of course.” Again, he slowly disengaged, and rolled onto his back, inviting Zinn to get between his legs, nudging the back of Zinn’s thighs with his heels to urge him along.

Zinn savored every warm, slippery inch as he pushed into Beau’s body once more, watching his face, feeling his back arch. He experimented with holding Beau in different places – gripping his hips to hold him down, grabbing him under his behind to hold him up. But it was when he slid his hands up the back of Beau's thighs and lifted them slightly that he realized he'd found the right thing. As he hoisted Beau's legs up, one by one, he discovered he could angle himself in deeper. So he raised them all the way up, until Beau's ankles rested on Zinn's shoulders, with Zinn's arms wrapped around Beau's knees. He trembled as he sank even further inside, shockingly deep.

"That's hitting it," Beau groaned, and when Zinn recovered his bearings and resumed his steady thrusting, Beau grunted, "You can do it a little faster now. And harder. Oh, *harder*." He was falling apart, surrendering to Zinn entirely. In the interest of servicing Beau properly, muscles Zinn hadn't even known he had were being overtaxed to the point of numbness, but he refused to interrupt the rhythm of his fluid thrusts.

He worked himself smoothly but relentlessly in and out of Beau's eager, unresisting body. Beau was yelling now, stroking himself, chanting "Fuck me, fuck me" under his breath. Obeying his orders, Zinn kept up his brutal pace, and Beau cried out, "Oh, fuck, Zinn, you're making me come." He thrashed and hollered his way through an astounding climax, squeezing reflexively around Zinn's cock. It would have been mesmerizing to watch and feel any human working through their orgasm, but Beau was so beautiful, Zinn wanted the moment to last forever, so he would never have to stop enjoying it.

But there was a new feeling creeping up on Zinn now. He began to feel very strange all over, like something was rolling around in his gut and his hips. He was trying to keep things going smoothly, to anticipate possible outcomes, so he asked, "When I ejaculate... is it alright to do that inside you?"

Beau groaned, "Yes. Just keep doing what you're doing, and that's what will happen."

"Oh," Zinn gasped, "it feels like too much, though."

"Zinn, do what I say. Push up deep and put everything you've got in me."

Zinn wanted so badly to make Beau happy. He rolled his hips and grabbed Beau's behind and pushed and pushed, and it came; the deep, warm tingle was sparked into an inferno, and he groaned, "I'm doing it!"

Reaching orgasm while sweetly confined by Beau's body was the most incredible thing Zinn had ever experienced. He climaxed for so long, so intensely, he thought he might not survive it, and cried out with gorgeous anguish. Beneath him, Beau relaxed into it, and sighed. "That's it, nice and deep inside me."

Zinn could feel the hard spurts as they left him, each one weaker than the last but all of them hot and pleasant, and all through them he uttered a final, plaintive vowel. Long after he had emptied himself, he continued to pump, hoping to provoke a little more; those pulses had felt so good. But he was forced to give up, as the hard tremors faded from his limbs. Then he collapsed entirely, his arms hanging limply along his sides and his face pressed against Beau's sternum.

After a few deep breaths and a moment of blank-mindedness, he raised his head, but to move was too much work, so he rested his head and let his body go slack again. It was quite comfortable where he was, anyway; damp in places, but he could listen to Beau's heartbeat as it slowed and steadied, and feel himself lifted by each of Beau's big, satisfied sighs.

"Beau," Zinn panted. "I put it in you, like you told me."

"Yes," Beau said. "Well done."

In the silence, Zinn breathed in the strong, pleasant smell of their fucking, and thought about some of the things that had just happened, how it had been so intense he could barely breathe, but how Beau had just kept asking for more. He felt like he could go again very soon, if Beau was also willing and able. He wiggled as if to cuddle closer, despite the fact that he was on top of Beau, and physically unable to actually get any nearer. "How soon can we do it again?" he asked.

Beau laughed weakly, but did not answer, just stroked Zinn's back. It was quiet now. Zinn pondered how beautiful and ridiculous it was that you could join your body with another person's like that, and do what they had just done. He had not thought he would ever find the right person for him, the right Trevellian with whom he would feel joyous harmony. But what had this been, if it wasn't joy? He was so lucky to have met Beau.

Zinn remembered then that this, their first night together, was also to be their last, and his heart sank. "I don't want you to go," he said, pressing his face into Beau's chest.

Beau squeezed him tight. "I don't want to go either, but I have to."

Zinn rolled his overworked, aching body over, so that he was stretched alongside Beau, and played with the hair on Beau's chest as he lamented, "I don't think I'll ever find anyone as wonderful as you."

Beau chuckled. "I won't say that that's not true, because I am pretty great, but I'll be back."

"Will you really?" Zinn looked up, and tucked his head under Beau's chin.

"How could I stay away? And until then, I'll send you messages as often as I can."

"Every day?" Zinn sat up now, looking Beau in the eye.

"I'll try," Beau insisted.

"I want to know that you're doing alright."

"I know. But I told you, I'll be fine."

Zinn laid down again, feeling the muscles in Beau's arms. "How much longer can you stay?"

"A few more hours, yet."

"I'll stay up with you, until you have to go."

"Naw, don't do that. Fall asleep here in my arms, and I'll slip out and go when I have to. That'll be easier than saying goodbye."

Beau guided Zinn onto his other side and cuddled up behind him, so his back was pressed to Beau's chest. Zinn sighed as Beau's big arms enveloped him. Zinn closed his eyes. "Maybe you're right," he said. He wanted to stay awake as long as possible, to enjoy every moment of Beau's embrace, but he was so sleepy, and he just felt so safe and satisfied, and Beau was keeping him so warm and cozy...

When Zinn woke up, Beau was gone.

Days went by. Zinn continued to think about Beau all the time. He spent hours on his holoreader, searching for all the information he could find about the Dropol War. Trevellian sources didn't feature many stories about it; though the planet was hosting tens of thousands of humans on their way to fight in it, the war itself was a territorial conflict that did not quite involve them. Every day, Zinn scrounged up all the newest articles, searching for any sign that the war situation might be improving, any hint that Beau's duties would be over and he would be free to return to Trevell. But every report was so vague, so dry and unconcerned.

Weeks went by. Beau still occupied Zinn's thoughts, but those thoughts became darker all the time. Where at first, Zinn would stroll past a restaurant and think, *I should take Beau there when he comes back*, more often he began to slump his shoulders and hang his head when he walked past anything that seemed lively or diverting, increasingly certain that he would never enjoy that thing, or that place, because he couldn't ever enjoy it with Beau.

Zinn did not want to consider the possibility that Beau had died in the war. It was too tragic and too senseless to contemplate. But refusing to believe that Beau was dead left only one other possibility: that Beau had lied to him, that everything that Plax had said had been correct, and that this suffering was Zinn's punishment for ignoring the warning.

Months went by. On the darkest days, the days when he had trouble getting out of bed in the morning, or when he went to bed hours early because he couldn't think of anything better he might do, Zinn was paralyzed with regret about what he and Beau had done together. He should never have gone to bed with a human. He should have settled for nothing less than an appropriate Trevellian mate, like Plax had said. Now he was a miserable wretch, because he'd loved a human who was gone to some other planet without a care. What a fool he'd been.

All along, Blye, Vollo and Flid begged him to share what had happened that was making him so sad all the time. They had always known Zinn to be quiet and shy, but never melancholy. Never leaving a meal half-eaten because he had no appetite. Never blank-faced when someone made a joke. But Zinn refused to talk about what had happened. The only thing that could make the situation worse, he reasoned, would be if he admitted that he'd gone to bed with a human.

Beau is never coming back for you, he began to think, constantly. *He never intended to. He was a nasty human who snatched up the most gullible Trevellian he could find. He probably never even really liked the League, he just pretended.*

Zinn couldn't read League books anymore. A new League movie was released, with an all-new cast, but he did not go to see it. It was too painful, because it reminded him of Beau. He watched other things, read other books.

One day, Blye invited him to the city aquarium, and they took pictures of the sea creatures. Blye insisted that Zinn take pictures of him imitating the strangely-shaped mouths of some of the fish, and Zinn couldn't help but laugh at this. Afterward, they saw a movie about Lorr, the Trevellian who first explored the planet's frozen northern continent five hundred years ago, and the climactic scene was so suspenseful, Zinn didn't think about Beau for ten whole minutes.

The next day, it was easier to get out of bed. Zinn wanted to go to the library to get some books about Lorr. Then he was back at work, in the cafeteria at lunch, telling Blye, Vollo, and Flid all the new things he'd learned.

"Lorr always took three books with him, wherever he traveled," Zinn told them. "The *Epic of Glef*, the *Book of Trevellian Verse*, and *The Death Of Thur*."

"Stop listing books, Zinn, you're so boring!" Flid said. Everyone laughed, including Zinn, a little. Flid hugged Zinn tightly, rocking him back and forth. "Why are you so boring?" he said, trying to sound genuinely despondent. He pretended to wipe away a tear, crying softly, "Why do you like to list books?"

After work, they invited Zinn to play some card games at Blye's house – a recent weekly tradition which they had not stopped inviting Zinn to, no matter how many times he had politely demurred. This time, he accepted. No one was bothering to ask anymore why Zinn had been so sad, and so for the whole evening Zinn was not reminded that he had been sad.

Zinn still believed that he had made a mistake, but he stopped feeling like he couldn't go on because of it. As time passed, he thought of each day as one more day between himself and his foolishness. The Zinn who believed human lies was a different Zinn, not the person he was now.

When Zinn heard the notification on his pocket messenger, he ignored it for a while. He was busy making dinner, and anyway, it was probably something about one of his subscriptions or accounts. He didn't check the message until he was just about to go to bed.

The title of the message was *From your Intrepid Adventurer*.

Zinn clicked on the message to open it in full. It read:

My dearest, darling Zinn,

I'm sorry I didn't write sooner, but where they sent me was very remote, much more so than I was anticipating. However, with no interstellar communications to distract me, I had lots of time to read, and thanks to your generosity, I was able to finish all one hundred and seven League books. You'll be pleased to hear that I know who Melbo is now! I can't wait to talk to you about everything I read. I want to know how you feel about Zorb finding out that Rrodar was his father, and about how accurate their travels to the Great Remaking were.

I am currently on a ship leaving the Z Region. I've been told that we will be back on Trevell in three days. I'll come visit you the first chance I get, if that's alright? I'm so excited to see you again. I thought about you all the time, and it hurt so badly because I missed you so much, but it hurt worse to try not thinking of you. I'm sorry that I couldn't tell you where I was, but I'll be with you soon, and hopefully I can make it up to you.

Please have some snacks and the next League movie ready for me when I get there.

Love, Beau

Zinn tried to scroll further, hoping there were somehow more words from Beau, but the message was over. He whimpered and collapsed on the sofa. Could this be a cruel prank? No, there were all those references in the message to League things that only he and Beau knew about.

He read the whole thing again, or tried to, distracted by the pounding of his own heart, the buzzing in his brain. It was re-reading the sentence about Beau's imminent return that gave Zinn a final shock – three days? Three days from when? Zinn read the timestamp on the message. Despite the fact that Beau was on a travelling ship, if the ship's transmitter had been set to the Trevell calendar and clock, the timestamp should have been fairly accurate. Despite the fact that the message had only shown up on Zinn's pocket messenger an hour ago, the timestamp indicated that it had been sent–

There was a knock on the door, and Zinn dropped his messenger on the floor. He fell off the couch trying to roll off of it, and scrambled up to run for the door, nearly knocking himself out when he ran right into it. He flung the door open, and there stood Beau in a battered uniform, looking tired but happy, holding a paper bag from which emanated the most enticing odors, strong and complex.

"Hey," Beau said, smiling sheepishly. Zinn was frozen in shock, his mouth hanging open. Beau said, "You didn't respond to my message, so I thought maybe you didn't want to see me again. But I figured if I brought you something from the Forty-Two, some of the regular menu items, maybe I could change your mind?"

Zinn wasn't looking at the bag at all, only at Beau's sweet face. His clenched fists covered his irrepressible grin. He was shaking all over.

Beau grinned back, hope in his eyes. "Is that a Yes?"

ACKNOWLEDGMENTS

The author would like to thank Lee Douglass and Colleen Veillon of Carnation Books; her editor, Natalia Savana Munoz; and anyone else who has ever supported her by telling her, "Excellent smut, keep up the good work!"

ABOUT THE AUTHOR

Berlynn Wohl divides her time between Seattle and the Internet. She will continue writing until someone stops her.

ABOUT CARNATION BOOKS

Carnation Books is a fandom-powered publisher of the best in inclusive fiction. Founded in 2016, Carnation Books is at the forefront of new author discovery. Visit carnationbooks.com to learn more, and to sign up for our story-filled newsletter!

PRAISE FOR DREAMS AND MACHINES...

Amazon readers say:

"Like a good album, this anthology has something for many moods. Silly antics? Existential warmth? Tangled melancholy? Whichever particular flavor you like, there's a story to spice it up."

"Interesting, thought provoking and just really hot."

"It's funny, sexy, and smart, and the short stories are great for a quick read whenever you need something smutty, or a good laugh."

Visit CarnationBooks.com for more information about this fantastic title by Berlynn Wohl!

PRAISE FOR OH, EARTHMAN!

Amazon readers say:

"Hot, thought provoking, and amusing in turns. Each story is a unique world unto itself."

"A sci-fi Decameron of a sort...highly recommended if you like to explore the mating rituals of humans (and some other species)."

"One story made my jaw drop, my eyes widen in shock, and my heart tried to beat out of my chest, I thought I knew what was coming, but I was wrong. Another had me cooing in delight at how sweet it was, and quite a few had me sweating like a sinner in church."

Visit CarnationBooks.com for more information about this fantastic title by Berlynn Wohl!

CPSIA information can be obtained
at www.ICGtesting.com
Printed in the USA
LVHW091122041119
636250LV00004B/1009/P

9 781948 272223